Joygirl 636

Jennifer Jade Benfield

Outskirts Press, Inc.
Denver, Colorado

Joygirl 636
All Rights Reserved.
Copyright © 2009 Jennifer Jade Benfield
V4.0R1.1

Outskirts Press, Inc.
http://www.outskirtspress.com

ISBN: 978-1-4327-1205-1

Outskirts Press and the "OP" logo are trademarks belonging to Outskirts Press, Inc.

PRINTED IN THE UNITED STATES OF AMERICA

DEDICATION

Dedicated to my children, Justin and Jennifer
who love me unconditionally
and
to Patrick for believing in me
to make this book possible

INTRODUCTION

Do you know what your spouse is doing on the internet?

Have you ever wondered what is so damn interesting to keep them mesmerized by their monitor and pecking at the keyboard for hours at a time?

Do they treat you like the enemy anytime you walk into the room or ask to join them on the computer?

Are they defensive if you ask what they are doing or who they are chatting with?

Are you blocked with passwords and firewalls from using the computer?

If you answered yes to any of the above questions, <u>*you have reason to be concerned.*</u>

The **"pseudo world"** of the internet is so addictive. Why? You can pretend to be anyone you want to be or pretend to live anywhere in the world.

There is no sense of time, no bills to pay and all the cyber sex you want.

You ask, "How do you know this?"

I lived it....

The true story I am about to share with you actually happened in 2003 and is so bizarre you won't believe it – the <u>first time</u> you read it. And you WILL read it over -perhaps again and again.

For if you have a computer in your home, at some time; you also will live my story.

CHAPTER 1
The Conversation

Jade1654: When you are finished with your spades game, could we talk about Tom?

Joygirl636: yes

Jade1654: Thank you very much. I just have some unresolved issues with him and I do not mean any harm to you.

Joygirl636: i understand that.

Jade1654: I loved him very much and after I had my stroke, it was a lot for me to handle that he told me he didn't love me anymore.

Joygirl636: you had a stroke?

Jade1654: 8-21-02

Joygirl636: damage?

Jade1654: For a while there was, but I got my speech back that was slurring. I still lose my balance sometimes, but getting better as long as I don't close my eyes and try to turn around.

Joygirl636: Jade, didn't YOU leave him?

Jade1654: He told me he didn't love me anymore and didn't want me around. What would you have done?

Joygirl636: left

Jade1654: Then I begged him to seek counseling with me and to try to work things out. He said he wasn't interested.

Jade1654: I broke down and begged.

Jade1654: I think I will always love him despite how badly I hurt but I was not productive to him any longer.

Jade1654: Did he tell you we owned a business together?

Joygirl636: yes. i do not intend to meet him until there is a divorce- this bothers me. i did not know he was still married when we started talking.

Jade1654: I didn't leave until October 3, 2002 and he has been with me on several occasions since then. I have it written down on my calendar and have witnesses.

Jade1654: We do not have separation papers as he has refused to sign the three sets I have given him.

Jade1654: Do you live close?

Joygirl636: no

Jade1654: Where do you live?

Joygirl636: states away

Jade1654: Missouri?

Joygirl636: yes

Joygirl636: he told me there were papers and that is why he moved in with his mom and dad.

Jade1654: NO, he owns his own home. He moved in with his parents so his mom could take care of his boys on the weekend he has them and she cooks and cleans for him most likely. There is no reason why he can't live in his own trailer.

Joygirl636: i want you to do me a favor?

Jade1654: What dear? I do not want you to get hurt the way I did.

Joygirl636: tell him we had this talk and that i don't want to talk to him!

Jade1654: I would love to call you and talk to you more about the situation.

Joygirl636: i am sorry.

Jade1654: You really need to know what kind of snake he has turned into.

Joygirl636: i think i know.

Jade1654: and I do not mean to do this to hurt you but he has hurt three of us women actually the same way.

Joygirl636: i told him to try counseling

Jade1654: I miss his boys terribly.

Joygirl636: jade, I am young.....this will not hurt for long! Hell, I can go out tonite and find some-one.....thank u.

Jade1654: He has even hit on my girlfriends

Jade1654: Age?

Joygirl636: i know the boys like you....they told me so

Joygirl636: 21

Joygirl636: i know he is a flirt

Jade1654: Did he tell you how old I was?

Joygirl636: how old?

Jade1654: He is a WOMANISER.....

Jade1654: but people tell me I look much younger than he because of his gray hair

Joygirl636: i asked to see a picture of u

Jade1654: and?

Joygirl636: he wouldn't

Jade1654: It is on my profile.

Joygirl636: i am glad we had this talk.

Jade1654: I wanted to talk to you the other night when the two of you were on but he wouldn't leave.

Joygirl636: i told him u and I would talk some day.

Jade1654: We girls gotta look out for one another

Joygirl636: yes we do

Jade1654: So what did he say about me? I won't tell him, I just need to know.

Joygirl636: that u used him.....i don't care if you tell the F_____.

Jade1654: I never used him....I loved him with all my heart and I am crying as we speak because I still love him despite all he has done to me.....he broke my heart.

Joygirl636: jade you have nothing to worry about here!!!!!

Jade1654: I devoted my whole life to him and his boys after we got married.

Joygirl636: so sorry

Jade1654: Well it is over between him and me as he has dumped me to move on but I did not want you to not know about him. Keep this to yourself but I have proof. Did he tell you he was bi and a cross dresser?

Joygirl636: lol

Joygirl636: no

Joygirl636: damn

Joygirl636: i believe u

Jade1654: Yeah a lot of this stuff came out after we got married.

Joygirl636: i knew there was something

Jade1654: how?

Jade1654: too smooth?

Joygirl636: yeah

Joygirl636: and i know smooth

Jade1654: He is quite the talker when he wants something.

Joygirl636: he thinks

Jade1654: I was dating a guy for years on/off when I met Tom. Thank God you are smarter than I as I believed all his crap and hurt a very nice man.

Joygirl636: he is just an old navy whore

Jade1654: The guy has talked to me several times since he found out I am living alone and he told me he was sorry I got hurt so badly. I told him it should be me apologizing for the way I hurt him. He said that we had an understanding that if either one of us found someone that we thought would make them happier then to go for it.

Jade1654: I have lost thirty two pounds over this. Needed to lose the weight but not to the point of suicide.

Joygirl636: jade you take good care of urself. u go out and have fun! show him!

Jade1654: Thank you for talking to me. He said you were just a girl he talks with.

Joygirl636: i am so damn mad, but i want to laugh at the same time.

Joygirl636: LOL

Jade1654: He tells everyone I just walked out and that is not the way it happened.

Joygirl636: yeah, that is what he tells

Jade1654: That is why I have been on here so much-trying to find you to talk

Joygirl636: i knew u would

Joygirl636: i told him u would

Jade1654: That first night I found the two of you in that spades room- he called me shortly after that.

Joygirl636: lol

Jade1654: Trying to cover his self

Joygirl636: i told him off good that night

Jade1654: What did you say?

Joygirl636: i just told him that he forgot he was married and that I just remembered and was done!

Jade1654: You know he would sit at the computer for hours at a time, just like he did that Sunday the race was on. He would be on that computer and not say a word to me for five hours unless I asked him for something to drink- just pecking away at the computer and smirking every once in a while. When I would ask him what he was snickering about he would just look at me with the look to just drop dead.

Joygirl636: is he real skinny?

Jade1654: He seems to conveniently forget he is married until one of my friends will see him and give him heck over it.

Jade1654: He is 6' 2", 190 lbs. not very muscular. Compared to the guy I was seeing who 6' 4", 230 lbs and solid muscle-there is not much comparison there.

Joygirl636: lol

Joygirl636: damn girl - what is wrong with you?

Jade1654: Tom just said all the right things and Sam wasn't ready for a serious relationship. He had been hurt in a previous marriage and like an idiot, I thought Sam didn't care.

Jade1654: yeah, damn girl is right. Sam is such an endearing person who was hurt deeply and after two years I felt our relationship would always be just good buddies. So, I decided to move on with my life.

Jade1654: Kicking myself still.

Joygirl636: well

Joygirl636: we can do better

Jade1654: YES WE CAN

Joygirl636: i promise- this is over on this end......

Jade1654: The decision is up to you. I am not asking you to end it but I thought you should know the truth and the whole story.

Joygirl636: i thank u

Jade1654: He has three wives he has screwed over now

Joygirl636: 3..............i thought just 2?

Jade1654: LMAO..........he is such a liar.

Jade1654: Gees...........got married at 20 and divorced at 22 or there about; then there was Beth (Casey and Carl's mom) and he ran on her also. But I didn't know all of this until after I left him and started digging around to find out what makes him tick. We married in '99 on the day of the anniversary of my Mom's death.

Jade1654: he told me it was going to be a happy day from then on.

Joygirl636: he never told me about the first one

Jade1654: Her name is Carrie.

Joygirl636: lol

Joygirl636: mmmmm mmmmmmmmmm mmmmmmmmmm

Jade1654: Does he know the truth? Was he planning on taking a trip to Texas and you meet him there?

Joygirl636: i heard a lot of anger in his voice at times....like he could be mean

Joygirl636: no, Texas was never mentioned

Joygirl636: i told him he had to be divorced

Jade1654: OH YES, he has a terrible temper. He is the only boy and the youngest child......spoiled absolutely rotten and he can really pitch a fit.

Jade1654: So you have talked to him on the phone?

Joygirl636: yes

Jade1654: he lied to me then

Joygirl636: mmmm mmmmm

Jade1654: Said you only played spades together.

Joygirl636: DAMN LIAR

Joygirl636: have you been with him since the separation?

Jade1654: Are you heybaby636 also?

Joygirl636: yeah

Jade1654: yes I have been with him.

Joygirl636: I KNEW IT!!

Jade1654: The last time was Feb. The boys were the ones who told me about you.

Joygirl636: i knew it......he lied to me and i knew eventually they would tell you as they like you a lot.

Jade1654: Did you see him on the computer night before last on messenger when was idle? "Just sittin' here waiting for my baby."

Jade1654: I had a friend write him and ask him who the "baby" was as that was what he called me all the time.

Joygirl636: no, I didn't see that.

Joygirl636: M---------F---------LOL

Jade1654: He calls you baby all the time?

Jade1654: Guess he doesn't have to remember any names that way.

Joygirl636: LOL

Jade1654: and yours is by the way?

Joygirl636: Jennifer

Jade1654: OMG- that is my and my daughter's name

Joygirl636: WHAT?

Jade1654: true!

Joygirl636: mmmmmmmmmm

Joygirl636: LOL

Jade1654: How did he find you?

Joygirl636: it was like two years ago. i was playing poker...i was still in school

Joygirl636: we were just friends

Jade1654: That lying bastard....He told me he met you online in November

Joygirl636: then in September he messengers me and starts talking all this shit

Joygirl636: believe me

Joygirl636: no reason to lie here

Jade1654: I know, I am just broken hearted for all the time he has been on and soooo secretive when he was talking to you

Jade1654: we used to share all that together

Joygirl636: i am so sorry

Jade1654: Then sometime back before I left he got real defensive and pass worded EVERYTHING. I couldn't even get past turning it on.

Jade1654: You just don't know how badly this man hurt me.

Joygirl636: No I don't

Jade1654: And he made it feel it was all my fault.

Joygirl636: i don't intend to go there

Joygirl636: i always thought it was my job he liked

Joygirl636: and my age

Jade1654: which was?

Joygirl636: nurse- RN

Jade1654: Did he tell you that I owned a real

estate company?

Joygirl636: oh yes

Joygirl636: many, many times- he was obsessed at the thought of all the money you could have made selling real estate

Jade1654: then we financed my house and bought a restaurant and he bitched because I worked all the time

Joygirl636: and that HE BOUGHT you the restaurant and then a car lot with his retirement

Jade1654: Pardon my French--- F------liar as we mortgaged my house which is now in foreclosure.

Joygirl636: i have asked him if he gives you any support and he said sometimes

Jade1654: The car lot was his idea and he didn't help much with it

Jade1654: Liar

Joygirl636: and that u stole money from him and went out to shoot pool

Jade1654: OMG- what a liar he is. He gave me money to shoot pool and that was once a week at $10 to get me out of the house.

Joygirl636: he likes to spend money doesn't he?

Jade1654: well let's put it this way.....he bought a pool table from a friend of his that owns a pool room and we don't even have a space big enough to it in. The table stays at the guy's pool room until he "adds on the house" which will never happen.

Jade1654: he said he wanted me to shoot pool because we needed some space between us

Joygirl636: so he can dress up and use his web cam

Jade1654: Web cam? He must have bought that after I left. I didn't know he had one.

Joygirl636: LOL....sick son of a bitch

Joygirl636: i knew it

Joygirl636: he made fun of my saving

Jade1654: You have been talking to him for two years and he never mentioned he was married?

Joygirl636: the first time we met online....he was divorced he said

Jade1654: Where did you meet him and when?

Joygirl636: in the poker room, almost two years ago in August or June

Jade1654: We met October 13, 1998

Joygirl636: then?

Jade1654: married November 27, 1999

Joygirl636: then we went for months without speaking. i even deleted him off my friends list. hell, i deleted him all the time because I would get mad at him

Jade1654: We were back together when he wouldn't talk to you

Joygirl636: didn't know that. i was 20 when i met him on here. will be 22 July 8

Jade1654: did he tell you that he and I have the same birthday?

Joygirl636: NO

Jade1654: January 16

Joygirl636: he never told me that

Joygirl636: we fought a lot about u

Joygirl636: it always bothered me

Joygirl636: but the legal separation papers were in effect and the divorce would be final in October

Jade1654: NOPE

Jade1654: Was he planning to bring you back here?

Joygirl636: yeah- after the divorce

Jade1654: OMG

Joygirl636: LOL

Jade1654: This is blowing my mind

Joygirl636: i knew there was something. i knew it. i felt it

Jade1654: When did he talk to you about moving here?

Joygirl636: last November

Jade1654: As he led me to believe that we could possibly get back together until January

Jade1654: He was a member of a swapping site When I first met him. Then he talked me into doing it when we got together. But I hated it as I wanted a monogamous relationship. But it was his way of ex-tracurricular sex without cheating.

Joygirl636: well he better remain a member cause i don't want anything else to do with him.

Joygirl636: i know what i am going to do. what are you going to do?

Jade1654: I am still in shock right now but I do know that I won't go back to him now.

Joygirl636: i'm not

Joygirl636: i'm cool

Joygirl636: LOL

Joygirl636: hey, wish we could fix him up good

Joygirl636: why don't we play spades together some nite when we know he is on?

Jade1654: That would be so funny.

Joygirl636: LOL damn right

Joygirl636: he doesn't hit you does he?

Jade1654: He started to one day but he knows better than to try and hurt me.

Joygirl636: LOL good

Jade1654: He talked to me on the phone last night for almost an hour.

Joygirl636: what time?

Jade1654: Hold on- I will check caller ID

Joygirl636: OK

Jade1654: 10:55pm

Joygirl636: i knew this would happen. i told him it would

Jade1654: What did he say when I messengered you

the other night and you two sat in the spades room for the longest time?

Joygirl636: LOL......i left

Jade1654: I noticed and he just sat there waiting for me to say something to him

Joygirl636: and he called and i cussed him out and didn't talk to him for a few days

Joygirl636: i know he couldn't move when you came in that room and said something to us

Jade1654: I was such a pushover trying to please him all the time. Nothing was ever good enough and I never do anything right.

Joygirl636: he said he was shocked

Jade1654: Shocked that you cussed him out?

Joygirl636: no, when u came in the spades room- he didn't think you would find us in there so that way it was a way to communicate and have some fun too

Joygirl636: I private messengered him and asked if that was you

Jade1654: I have monitored you two for months

Joygirl636: REALLY

Jade1654: I have page after page of documents proving how much time he spends on the computer with you. He might have been able to block me from his laptop while we were still living together but he didn't think about me monitoring him after I left.

Joygirl636: hmmm

Jade1654: His mom said I was imagining things when we were together but now that he lives with her-she now knows. Hell, he even took over her recliner!

Joygirl636: his mom and dad both know now. his dad gets mad at him i think

Jade1654: His dad gets mad because Tom has responsibilities around the farm and with him on the computer or the phone with you; he is not living up to his responsibilities. Bob has done a lot for Tom and the more he does, the more Bob expects. I don't think his dad likes me very much as I try to get him to move around, walk and exercise some to help with his sugar diabetes and circulation. But all he wants to do is sit in his recliner, eat and watch television.

Joygirl636: he needs to do something

Joygirl636: he is eating himself to death

Jade1654: Tom had them so thoroughly convinced that I was the bad guy and now they won't talk to me

Joygirl636: and i hate to tell you this but Tom is not healthy

Jade1654: Bob is eating himself to death and Lacy is not helping with all the sugar and starches she is feeding him all the time

Joygirl636: i know

Jade1654: What is wrong with Tom?

Joygirl636: the man can't breathe good. haven't you noticed?

Jade1654: he had cytomegalovirus. I found it months after we met.

Joygirl636: what is that?

Jade1654: Hey you're the RN- you should know these things or at least have the pdr to look them up.

Joygirl636: oh yeah

Jade1654: He nearly died as the doctor kept prescribing antibiotics and he just kept getting worse. Finally, after several weeks of this, Tom couldn't even walk from the bedroom to the living room without being so give out he couldn't put his socks and shoes on. I got on the computer at night after work and would go through illnesses on the CDC until I found some that matched.

Joygirl636: he never mentioned it

Jade1654: The doctor didn't believe me but I demanded a blood test. I explained to the doctor that I had been on the computer and found matches for the symptoms he had. He thought I was crazy until he got the results back. They told me to take him off the antibiotics and I explained I had done that the week earlier and he had improved some. The antibiotics sped up the bacteria and it could have killed him.

Jade1654: I stayed out of work for about three weeks to take care of him.

Joygirl636: what r u going to do?

Joygirl636: how could u still want him after all of this?

Jade1654: Oh I will most likely file for divorce and he is gonna pay for all his lies, deceits and two timing cheating.

Joygirl636: i think i will messenger him when i get off here and just say F--- Y--.

Jade1654: I wonder how I could have fallen in love with such a person.

Joygirl636: i don't think i ever loved him-enjoyed his company.

Jade1654: Thank you for talking to me. I have proof and witnesses to back up everything I have told you.

Joygirl636: i don't doubt you

Jade1654: I didn't mean to do anything but let you know the REAL Tom.

Joygirl636: and i thank you

Jade1654: I just didn't want you to get hurt the way I did and he doesn't even care who he hurts.

Joygirl636: i am so glad i didn't meet him

Joygirl636: sooo glad

Jade1654: He was supposed to go to the neurologist's office with me the other day to find out the results from my MRI but he stood me up

Jade1654: If he is capable of dumping his wife after she is recovering from a stroke, what else is he capable of doing?

Joygirl636: anything absolutely- u know?

Jade1654: It was finally good to talk to you Jennifer and we will trip him up one night and play spades together.

Joygirl636: you too Jade...i actually feel relieved

Jade1654: Stay in touch and we will discuss anything BUT Tom

Joygirl636: we will get him good, lol

Jade1654: We will.

Joygirl636: just once then I don't want to waste any more time here

Jade1654: What would really flip him out is I three way call him while he is at work.

Joygirl636: OMG it would be interesting to hear how he treats you

Jade1654: That would really get him- then he would know he was busted for sure.

Joygirl636: he really needs to get busted

Jade1654: YES HE DOES

Joygirl636: yeeeeeeeessssssss, lol thank you

Jade1654: So stay in touch and I appreciate all of this.

Joygirl636: anytime

Jade1654: I knew there was a driving force behind him dumping me and it was his relationship with you.

Joygirl636: well.......

Jade1654: as everyone thought we had a great marriage

Joygirl636: he will be running back, LOL bet on it

Jade1654: Running back to nothing.

Jade1654: I cried so hard the other Sunday when I was there getting some of my things. I laid my face on his chest crying and his heart was racing. When I looked up at him and touched his face; he closed his eyes.

Joygirl636: i can't talk about that right now

Joygirl636: don't cry for him

Jade1654: Not any more. What hurts is to think about the way he did me with no conscious at all.

Joygirl636: do it anyway you want. i was smart and i am so thankful i didn't get involved with him

Jade1654: A lot smarter than I.

Jade1654: Would you have really moved here from Missouri having just met him off the internet?

Joygirl636: NO

Joygirl636: i told him he would get me down here and be hateful and then who would i have to turn to

Jade1654: You are right there.

Jade1654: I would ask you how he persuaded you so much but hell- I left my home since 1969 to move in with him!

Joygirl636: i was losing respect for him for some time now

Jade1654: There were so many days that we would not see each other as he refused to come home to eat before he went to work and he worked all the time trying to avoid me.

Joygirl636: and the age was something too

Joygirl636: he works all the time?

Joygirl636: i know

Jade1654: I am a workaholic too so I understood the work part but we never went anywhere when we were off or took a vacation. Even before you came into the picture, he always said we couldn't afford it or he didn't have the time.

Joygirl636: i'm a workaholic too

Jade1654: He is running from himself.

Joygirl636: i wonder what is wrong with him?

Jade1654: He wrote me one day that "his life was such a mess."

Joygirl636: his father not giving him his name

Joygirl636: there is something deep bothering him

Jade1654: I told him that until he got counseling to understand, Tom and all the stuff going on around him; he would always be a mess.

Jade1654: I always asked him to find out the truth as the uncertainty of who his real father was bothered him. But you can look at Bob and Tom and they certainly look like father and son.

Jade1654: Bob just treats him like a slave at times-pushes him-expects more time than Tom can give with a full time job and family too. There are some things Bob could do if he would just get off his dead ass and do it.

Joygirl636: i know

Jade1654: After we got married, it would have been really nice if Bob would have done that to give us a little more time together. Not a good way to start out a marriage by just passing in the hallway.

Jade1654: I told him last night, as I always do, that I was worried about him working so much.

Joygirl636: he will have a heart attack, watch, you will see

Jade1654: I don't wish him any ill will- just don't wish him anything at this point.

Joygirl636: just be glad it is over

Jade1654: I understand now-it makes sense. I can't believe he hid it from me for so long. I had no clue. How stupid I was to ever believe him about anything. It was all a lie.

Joygirl636: he did do that to you and still lied to me

Jade1654: and men wonder why we don't trust them

Jade1654: So when he was playing you on the computer two years ago-where did he say I was?

Joygirl636: i lived in a dorm....for 3 years.....my friends went through everything! i watched and listened

Joygirl636: i thought he was just divorced from Beth

Jade1654: OMG what a liar!

Joygirl636: he told me he was divorced

Jade1654: And then remarried between the times you last spoke two years ago. And now- it doesn't add up what you are telling me.

Joygirl636: he likes playing with fire doesn't he? LOL

Joygirl636: HE IS HERE!!!!!!!!!

Jade1654: REALLY?

Joygirl636: gonna messenger him, ok?

Jade1654: Sure, let me know what goes on. be sure to send it to me when you're finished.

Joygirl636: just called him a M--------F---

Jade1654: LOL

Joygirl636: asked him if he had a good talk with u last nite

Jade1654: what did he say?

Jade1654: He now knows that you and I have talked to have known that?

Joygirl636: OK

Joygirl636: just called him a sick F---

Joygirl636: LOL

Joygirl636: Gotta go

Joygirl636: LOL

Joygirl636: bye

Joygirl636: bye

Joygirl636: take care

Jade1654: He said that or are you telling me that?

Joygirl636: i said that to him

Joygirl636: sick bi F---...i am waiting for my phone to ring now

Jade1654: What did he say about the phone call last night?

Joygirl636: he denied it

Joygirl636: what is this?

Joygirl636: what do you mean?

Jade1654: This is so funny! He thinks he is such a player.....

Jade1654: Back in December and January I would have taken him back in a heart beat. I begged and pleaded with him for us to go to counseling, but not now.

CHAPTER 2

The Realization

Not long after the internet chat with Joygirl, the phone rang.

Guess who- you got it- TOM!

He asked what I was doing. I very bluntly but calmly told him, "*laundry*."

Then he asked if I was doing anything else. "*Talking to Joygirl636.*"

It suddenly got very quiet. I don't know if he thought I wouldn't admit to talking with her or he expected me to blow up and lose my temper.

"*What did you two talk about?*"

"*We spoke of a lot things- a lot can come out in two and a half hours of conversation. But I saved it if you want to read it as I have nothing to hide.*" I knew that would push some buttons as he knew I would stop at nothing when there is a mystery involved.

The reality of monitoring them the past few months had come to a head. It was time for answers. But would I get any?

"Whatever you said to her has made her so angry- she won't talk to me."

"Let's try some truth here Tom. It's not so much what I said but what you have done- according to her."

He had NO right to be angry as it was he who had deceived. Technically, **I was still his wife and I, before anyone, deserved some answers.**

"I can't really talk right now. I'm at mom's; but, I will call you back when I get to work and things slow down enough for me to take a break."

I knew he was stalling for time. He needed to talk to Joygirl and smooth things over with her. I paced back and forth across the floor until I couldn't take it any longer. I called a friend of mine, Rita. She had been helping me monitor Tom and Joygirl all along.

It was easy to see the spades games on yahoo by looking at their games history. But to actually catch them online you had to search each individual game room and check the tables. I had only found them once but I was booted from the table before I could say anything.

Rita was going through a difficult separation also

so we bonded quite quickly when we became friends. She asked what we had discussed. Too much info and so little time, as you read from the last chapter, so I emailed the conversation to her.

The whole time she was reading the attachment, she just repeated over and over what a dog Tom was, but it hurt like hell for me to admit it.

"I just don't trust him. I just don't trust him. He is gonna hurt you again and again," she warned.

Call waiting beeped in. It was Tom. I promised Rita I would call her back if it wasn't too late. She made me promise I would call her back no matter what time it was to make sure I was ok.

The conversation was awkward. I knew the phone call from him the night before was initiated by my "popping in" on their spades game and catching them before I was booted from the table. Now that I had actually chatted with Joygirl, I wanted to see what kind of covering up he was going to try this time.

Oh hell, there is no reason to delve into the whole conversation. A woman can pry all she wants and a man is going to give the same answers instilled in them since birth.

Excuse me....pardon my French- the same BS lies!!!

You know the ones:

1. I don't know.
2. We're just friends.
3. I don't know what YOUR problem is.
4. I don't know what you're talking about.
5. I miss you....but.......

Yeah, yeah, blah, blah, blah..............

I wanted to learn every detail I could; so I played along to hear what explanation he concocted. But first, I turned my recorder on so I could play this BS over and over. He didn't offer an explanation but the only thing he asked for was dinner the next night to "sort things out." Anyway, it would be a free dinner at what used to be our favorite restaurant. **Manipulation #1**

What the hell was I thinking? My stomach was tied in knots as he tried to explain. After stumbling over himself several times, he asked if I would just take a ride with him. We ended up back at his trailer, which was evident he hadn't been in much since moving in with his mom. It was cluttered from end to end, looking much like an abandonment of foreclosure. The only clear place to chat conveniently was the bed of the second bedroom and it been stripped of its sheets**Manipulation#2**

I don't know what situation he thought of at the time, but all of a sudden the crocodile tears just poured as he threw his arms around me and hugged me tighter than Dick's hatband. See, when Tom hugged me in the past, it felt like-well know what a dead fish handshake feels like....there ya go. Oh, he just cried and cried, in between telling me how I rescued him from a situation he had gotten so deep into he didn't know how to get out of. **Manipulation #3**

Did I hear him right? He was furious with me the day before because she refused to talk to him. Now, I am thrown off guard. So, I looked into those baby blues of his for some kind of "spiritual connection" I guess. OK- repeat again. The situation was????

As I walked around the room thinking, he walked up behind me putting his long arms around me. He whispered how much he had missed me and kissed me gently on the nape of my neck. **Manipulation #4**

"I missed holding you," he tearfully said.

To tell the truth, unfortunately I missed holding him even more but I wouldn't admit that to him. I had too much to find out.

He met her in a poker room two years ago when we separated the first time- oh yeah I forgot to mention we were separated before our first anniversary (November 2000 to refresh your memory). He had not spoken to her since we had gotten back together. That would explain the part where Joygirl said she hadn't spoken to him in months then deleted him off her messenger list.

Then, he messengered her one night after we separated the second time. Hmmm-two years had passed and he wanted me to believe he remembered her profile all that time- when he couldn't even tell you what he ate for breakfast that morning!

While he was talking, he fidgeted with my wedding ring which I had moved to my right hand since the day in January he told he wanted a divorce. Then he just started balling those tears again and said he was sorry. **Manipulation #5**

I hated to see him cry. OK now you can start screaming at me, if you haven't already. I'm an idiot, but that wedding ring was and still is sacred to me as it has the diamonds from my deceased Mother's wedding ring that was over 50 years old.

OMG! Give that man an Oscar as that had to be the best, damn performance of our entire relationship. His tears, his speech- he poured his little heart out to me as he had never done before.

Feeling the pressure from the upcoming **Ma-**

nipulation #6, I told him it was getting late and I needed to go home. OK now you can scream really loud because you guessed it- I gave in. Sex with Tom was never the problem. It was great when everything else was bad. Yes, I admit it. I was weak when it came to sex with Tom.

Manipulation #6 was a success on his part.

He had his boys, Anthony and Daniel, for the weekend and had planned to take them motorcycle riding at the track behind his house the next day. The boys and I were close and had a great relationship. **Manipulation #7**

The entire weekend went so smoothly. Why couldn't our marriage have been that nice when we were together?

Before you go into a rage- I hadn't forgotten the sleepless nights, my suicidal thoughts, endless crying or the fits of anger when I saw how much time he and Joygirl spent together on the internet.

After the boys left for church Sunday, we talked more. I wanted to know exactly how serious this relationship with Joygirl was; what the hell was going on and what his intentions were to resolve this mess. His story was pretty much the same as hers about how they met. Then it went a "little South."

He told me how she was just a sweet, naive, recent RN grad he had met in hold-em poker two years ago when she was just a student. After we had separated a while this second time, he was feeling lonely one night and tried to find her again to see how she was doing.

Now remind you- supposedly he had not "spoken" to her in two years. I asked him how he remembered her ID. He said her ID was catchy and he remembered it. Yes, I rolled my eyes in disbelief just like you did right now.

The two of them started playing spades together as she had an on-going bet with her friend, Lisa for $200. The first one to reach a 2000 ranking won. This is where it got interesting. He CLAIMED: she was the one inquiring on his marital status; what kind of job he had; how much money he made and how easy it would be for her to get an RN position in North Carolina.

OK, she supposedly was a twenty-two year old RN (which he had never met or even seen a picture of) interested in a thirty-nine year old man that she had only seen a picture from his profile and never met. And she was sweet talking him into moving her to North Carolina for a relationship?

Which head was he thinking with?

Weeks prior to all this revelation, I had taken my mounting evidence against Tom and Joygirl to my therapist, "Dr. Betty". She explained the fascination of a "pseudo" relationship on the internet. The second part of her interpretation I understood. This "girl", Tom had never met, appeared at a difficult time in Tom's life. Midlife crisis time had set in. He had doubted his purpose in life for two years- his parents tugging at him from one direction to do as they wanted him to do and I just wanting him to be the man HE wanted to be. He had constant mood swings, uncontrollable temper and had alienated everyone, including his boys by being on the internet for hours with Joygirl.

Forty was knocking on the door and here was this supposedly young, career oriented "beauty" (well he assumed) interested in him- a graying older man 18 years her senior.

I, being ten years older then Tom, two and two was beginning to look more like trouble- of the suing kind!

He ate up the ego stroking like it was his last meal.

Now, that what I thought was all out in the open, how were we going to deal with this situation?

I pleaded with Tom to think about things and to

go to therapy with me as a couple or perhaps he just needed to see her one on one for a few sessions then as a couple. He agreed to go as a couple.

I didn't completely move all my belongings back into the house nor did he move his; but we continued to try to work things out under one roof.

Monday night, he was back at work and I continued to soak up the facts I had learned over the weekend. He agreed he would have no contact with Joygirl. We agreed that I would write her and explain that we were back together but he wanted permission to write her an apology, if she would accept it.

CHAPTER 3

The Offline Message to Joygirl

Jade1654 (4:55am) I will only write you this once and not bother you but I have talked to Tom. Yes, we have talked and we are being honest about talking to each other.

He explained the relationship between the two of you was more casual and he feels badly for not being honest with you. I told him he should be for not being honest with BOTH of us. He knows he had hurt you badly and you had done nothing to be hurt in such a fashion. He would like a chance to explain and he asked me I would write asking your permission to talk to him.

He asked me if he really was a deceitful person. I said, "Yes, and manipulative also." I didn't cut him any slack. Guess he got back at himself- didn't he?

I guess you didn't say anything to me about how serious the relationship had gotten trying to spare my feelings.

Jade1654 (4:57am) But I demanded to know as I like honesty and everything out in the open. I never got angry as long as he was honest with me I asked for the truth. For me, it is easier dealing with the situation to know.

That is why I knew there was more to the situation than just spades and chatting buddies. You two were spending hours of time together on the internet. But, I knew Tom and knew there was more he was NOT telling me.

But, please talk to him, OK? I understand and won't be angry as long as everything is open.

Joygirl636: (2:59pm) Jade, I was always concerned about you. This caused many arguments. But I knew it was not right with him being married and I could not forget that fact!

Maybe the two of you can work something out. I would not want to go there!

It is nice of you to be concerned about him hurting me...it doesn't hurt that much. I have family..... many, many friends and have no problem getting dates! LOL...I thank you again.

I wish you the best in what ever you choose to do.

As far as "sicko" goes, men like him I can do without...LOL, I will be fine.

Jade1654: (3:00pm) Thank you for writing back. I have just always felt honesty was the best policy and he certainly was not honest....

He bent the truth!!

Now before you go off thinking I must be really stupid; surely, you don't think I believed all that CRAP from either side do you?

Hey, you know the old saying- I was born in the morning but just not this morning?

If I didn't go along with this little charade, how was I to find out what was really going on?

I suddenly realized that I hadn't called Rita back. She knew to give me some space hence her reason for not calling and checking on me.

When she heard my voice, she sighed a little knowing that I was willing to try and work things out with Tom. But I explained that I had vowed this marriage was my last and I had to try to make it work.

Her friendly reminder was- watch your back!

She reassured me (once more) that she would always be available, no matter what time of day or night, if I needed her.

CHAPTER 4
The Reconciliation

It was 7am when Tom got in from work. After the intense weekend and up all night at work, he just wanted to sleep. I attempted to sleep during the night to no avail and not much during the day either, so I got up and milled around the trailer.

The afternoon went by fast and soon it would be time for him to leave for work. We made it through the day without her name being brought up- how long would that last?

I sat in the living room wondering how I was going to deal with all of this but most of all if my health could stand dealing with all this drama. I heard him in the shower and get dressed but he hadn't come out into the living room yet.

A few minutes later, he emerged from the bedroom with a plastic bag of things- pictures, boxer underwear and a high school athletic t-shirt. She sent them to him at Christmas. There were also cards she sent him at Christmas and Valentines Day. He wanted me to ask her if she wanted the items back. Uh duh......what would you have done with them?

I didn't bother to tell him that she had already been on the net several times that day. I guess to see if he would be on.

Before he left for work, I made him take off all the passwords on his computer for me to have full access. He was not allowed to erase or move any files he may have on it either! He obliged. Well it appeared he was making an effort. Not gonna trust him this easily.....

He hadn't deleted the messages back and forth between him and Joygirl so I spent the afternoon reading. It was interesting read. Some of it was quite comical the dialogue between a thirty-nine year old man and a supposed twenty-one year old woman. Mushy stuff he had never hinted around me and little "kissy faces" all over the place. It was as if he had reverted back to a kid in high school. Now I am very romantic, but he had never shown that side of him to me. How did she pull that out of him?

It was late in the evening when I finally finished

reading the messages when she signed on. I guess she thought he was on or hoping I would be on to play mind games with me.

**I will warn you that the remaining part of this chapter is long and nothing but internet chat format, like the first chapter. And like the first chapter, if you skip or skipped it, you will miss some key information.

SO PAY CLOSE ATTENTION

Jade1654:(11:00pm) Tom wanted me to tell you that he is sorry for the way things turned out. He feels horrible as he should. He does not want you to feel used and feels he has lost a very good friend. He says he respects you very much.

I don't mind the two of you talking for closure, as long as everything is out in the open. He has deleted you from his friends list and won't bother you unless you want to talk to him. He says he will not cause any trouble for you or your mother as he respects you too much for that.

Joygirl636: Jade I have nothing to say to him. Nothing.

Jade1654: I understand totally. I don't know if I will ever trust him again and really don't know of I can go through this after what he had done. The

Lord says to forgive but I don't know I can forget. We talked about it last night. Men think wrong.

Joygirl636: I have two brothers who are complete Romeos. I learned the game early and know people very well.

Jade1654: One thing Tom is not...no matter how much he tries; but, he is no player. He doesn't do that well at all.

Joygirl636: LOL

No he doesn't
I always knew something wasn't right.
I always asked about you.
Always

Jade1654: This is nothing against you-please understand. But I think he just got wrapped up in the situation with him being alone.

Joygirl636: I know and I just ended a relationship.

Jade1654: And you were very good to Tom.

Joygirl636: Well, he had never seen the bad side of me and I have one.

Jade1654: I got into a similar situation when I was nineteen and I know that it hurts.

Joygirl636: I am ok

Jade1654: He did exactly what you said-he

asked me to come back home just like you said.

Joygirl636: I knew he would as he did talk about you all the time. We did fight a lot about that-he didn't seem to be over you.

Jade1654: But I told him I didn't trust him and he would have to earn that back.

Joygirl636: I wish you two lots of luck. You will need it. But u know. He has always been proud of you in a way- I pick up on that. But now that I think about it, I can't decide if it was you or the money he thought you could make. He said you were very talented when it came to making money. Worked very hard and an entrepreneur, very gutsy and passionate about what you believed in.

Jade1654: I didn't write to break you two up but to seek the truth. He showed me your pictures today.

Joygirl636: I haven't looked at urs yet and I thank you for fighting for your man. He wasn't planning to do anything with me anyway. I don't think.

Jade1654: The profile picture is horrible. My hair has grown out longer and I have lost weight. But I still get a lot of comments from friends that it is not bad for an "older broad."

Joygirl636: an older broad? Yes, I remember. Well I know he was crazy about you at one time.

It was if she was thinking out loud at that moment. I picked up on the fact she didn't remember how old I was and made a note.

Jade1654: Do you want me to send the pictures back to you?

Joygirl636: No just tear them up and throw them away. No one has noticed them missing.

Jade1654: Missing???????

There was no response. Perhaps this will all start tying together if I chat with her some more.

Jade1654: I will tell him I need them.

Joygirl636: JUST THROW THEM AWAY......

Now when you send something in UPPER CASE on the net, it means you are screaming. So my keeping the pictures irritated her.

Jade1654: You are a sweet person just like he said.

Joygirl636: I know...that is my nature, LOL.

Jade1654: I tried to explain to him why you would not want to remain friends with him from a woman's point of view but you know men.....

Joygirl636: He is no friend of mine. I have plenty.

Jade1654: I understand.

Joygirl636: Take care of urself. And try to work it out with him. I won't bother you any more.

Jade1654: I will try to make an honest effort and I will not bother you either. I do appreciate your honesty and sorry we had to meet like this.

Joygirl636: it's cool. I feel good inside. Married men are not my game. I learned.

Jade1654: Perhaps under other circumstances, we could have been friends.

Joygirl636: yeah

> I let a good one go.
> Not married, LOL.

Jade1654: Any chance of getting him back?

Joygirl636: nah and I don't want him back....guess he wasn't what I wanted or I wouldn't have let him go.

Jade1654: I lost my bf of five years to another girl in high school when he cheated on me and got her pregnant. He died at age thirty still telling me he married the wrong woman.

Joygirl636: damn....I lost my first in a car wreck.

Jade1654: It is so hard for me to take still....I still put flowers on his grave and tell him I wished things could have turned out differently.

Joygirl636: I used to put flowers on his grave and tell him I was sorry he had to miss so much in life.

Jade1654: I can relate.

Joygirl636 Damn he was handsome, LOL

I will meet someone.
They are a dime a dozen.

Jade1654: How many pictures were there? So, he doesn't try to pull a fast one.

Joygirl636: 3

Jade1654: OK he is telling the truth for a change then

Joygirl636: Wouldn't you hate to be like that? mmmm mmmm mmmm

Jade1654: I didn't want to get married right away as I told him he had to earn my trust. When I married this time, it would be my last.

Joygirl636: I know it started out good. He told me that.

Jade1654: He told me he sent you a Christmas card and a Valentine's card. So you did mean something to him as he never did that for me while we were dating or married!

Joygirl636: I didn't want to do the gift thing. But he insisted so I put a $10 limit on it. Of course, he didn't listen.

Jade1654: he never does.

Joygirl636: I feel sorry for him in a way. Maybe you can make him happy after all.

Jade1654: He said he saw a lot of me in you. That is what attracted him to you-perhaps just a younger version of me.

Joygirl636: I do feel guilty even though you told me not to. And yes, I do feel misled. Oh well, life goes on and on-and gets better.

Jade1654: I don't know that it will work as we have tried so many times before. It is like he doesn't know what he wants. He has everything a man could want. Comfortable home, great boys, a wife that adores him and is good to him, parents that spoiled him rotten and he still pulls this crap.

Joygirl636: LOL, he almost didn't make it the first time. I knew something. No second chance here. He is married. I deserve better. It will come. I know it will. I am young and have my while life ahead of me.

Jade1654: I didn't get married the first time until I was twenty two. I have been married several times and all for the wrong reasons, which I regret, but have remained friends with all of them. I had my son when I was twenty-eight and my daughter when I was thirty two.

Joygirl636: Damn, why so late? Why did you wait?

Jade1654: I never really wanted kids-was too full of myself to settle down to having children- too selfish! When I married Jim, I felt I could juggle career and family.

Joygirl636: I don't think I want children. I like to work too much to have kids.

Jade1654: Tom told me you are a diabetic.

Joygirl636: Yes I am. I worry about passing it on to my children.

Jade1654: It is really tough raising children and a career. I always felt guilty leaving my children in daycare. I spent so much time away from them. But when Jim and I divorced, I had to work. And I worked all the time just to make the ends barely meet. So there were no other options. They are twenty-one and seventeen this year.

Joygirl636: I knew how old they were as Tom told me. I asked about them.

Jade1654: He probably said my son was a pain.

Joygirl636: No, he likes him. Tom said the two of them have an ongoing pool feud.

Jade1654: WOW, I am surprised. Tom has two great boys but complete opposites. Anthony talked to me a long time while they rode motorcycles. He is going through the awkward teenage stage. Daniel is more the daredevil. He has a lot of Tom's stubbornness too. Tom pushes Anthony to be more outgoing and I told him to leave him alone and let him be his own man- what ever he wants to be. Trying to be someone you're not doesn't make a man.

Joygirl636: He has some nerve telling someone else how to grow up when he hasn't really experienced that phase yet- has he?

Jade1654: My mom died when I was expecting Justin- she never saw her first grandchild. My dad is now 73 and remarried and is happy.

Joygirl636: What a shame that your mom never got to experience her first. What a joy. Treasure your father. Hell my dad is still taking care of me. He worked hard all his life. I called him Daddy until he drew his last breath.

Jade1654: I still call mine Daddy too. He loves it when I kiss him on his cheek and tell him I love him in front of his customers.

Joygirl636: Yeah, I miss that so much. Mine left me a house in Florida. I haven't even been there to see it. My brother lives in there and takes care of it for me. My dad worked hard for all of us.

Jade1654: I hope this conversation is not bringing you down. If it is, I apologize and we can change the subject.

Joygirl636: It is but it is ok. It is nice to be able to talk to someone about it. Perhaps I will go to Florida, LOL.

Jade1654: They say it gets easier as times goes by but it really doesn't. Sometimes I try to recall my mom's voice or her laugh but it just doesn't come. Too much time has passed.

Jade1654: Get this though. My mom dies November 27th and the guy I dated for five years passed away November 27th the following year. Tom married me on November 27th vowing to make it a "happier time for now on" and we didn't even make it to our first anniversary when we separated.

Joygirl636: Damn, wonder what this November will bring? LOL....MMMMMMMMMMM

Jade1654: Tom said I suffered long enough and he wanted to make it a happy time from now on.

Joygirl636: As if he understands what suffering is....He eats like a pig!

Jade1654: What brought that up?

Joygirl636: LOL, I don't know. I am laughing so hard. It just came to me- my diabetic condition and his way of eating- all that junk food is going to kill him.

Jade1654: Well the eating habits are going back to my way of eating. I may be a big person but I still try to eat right. Oh, by the way, I made him a doctor's appointment and he agreed to go.

Joygirl636: I have no comment at this time about that. I could care less. Hey, I would like to go play a game of spades before bed-worked 16 hours today. Thank you for everything. I mean this. Glad it's over.

Jade1654: Can I ask you one question before you go please?

Joygirl636: Well you did ask nicely again. So, go ahead.

Jade1654: And please be honest as this is for my information only. Do you care for him more than you are letting on? I feel you are trying to protect my feelings. He told me that he told you he loved you.

Joygirl636: I liked him as a person first. Thought he was cool. Then we started talking and then talking a lot. Then I wanted him sexually. Then I had some feelings that were confusing to me.

Jade1654: Lust and love CAN be confusing.

Joygirl636: I guess. I have never been in love before so maybe I just got confused.

Jade1654: It is hard to separate sometimes. Tom asked me to marry him two weeks after we started dating. That is moving way too fast. Then he gave me a ring but we waited a year before we got married. I had my kids to consider.

Joygirl636: Was he good to them? I always wondered what kind of dad he would be with our kids.

Jade1654: Then we went through a family crisis and that is when all our troubles began. It was devastating.

Joygirl636: He never mentioned it so I don't know anything about that. I am going to see a doctor.

Jade1654: Doctor? Anything wrong?

Joygirl636: no silly....guess I should have phrased it a little differently. This guy has asked me out and dated my friend (roommate Edie)

Jade1654: What do you two do? Play spin the doctor or is she ok with you going out with one of her ex-boyfriends?

Joygirl636: She said he really wasn't her type but thought the two of us would get along great. She is just getting over a bad affair and doesn't really care. She got involved with a guy off the internet from Ohio. He moved down and everything-leaving his wife. I think his name was Robert. Anyway, once he moved here- she dumped him.

Jade1654: we'll never know- do us girls. You think your knight in shining armor arrives and it is just one lie on top of another one.

Joygirl636: Hell no. Is life always this hard?

Joygirl636: Do the good exceed the bad?

Jade1654: Yes it does. But life is also what you make of it. If you wish for lemons all the time, you get lemons. You must start changing your way of thinking. So, what about the doctor?

Joygirl636: you just made me smile thinking about him.

Jade1654: I am glad as I like to make people laugh and smile- it's my nature.

Joygirl636: He is going to my niece's ballgame with me, then to dinner.

Jade1654: Not to change the subject, but I have a doctor's appointment soon. Did Tom tell you that they suspect I have MS?

Joygirl636: Yes he did. Hate to hear that. Have u been tested?

Jade1654: I had another spinal tap about 5 weeks ago. They both came back positive.

Joygirl636: Damn. Think positive. You are strong.

Jade1654: I refuse to let it get me down. I am too active. But in a way, I can understand why Tom took the attitude he had about my illness. When I had my stroke, I imagined he didn't bargain for baggage at such a young age. But he failed to remember that he wasn't in the best of health after we started living together and I didn't complain about his health or dump him. I took care of him because I loved him.

Joygirl636: exactly

Jade1654: I did agree to sell my horse and that decision killed me.

Joygirl636: U have a horse? i knew you rode. Tom told me but I didn't know you had a horse.

Jade1654: I have enjoyed riding since the age of 5.

Joygirl636: I ride very badly. Damn Jade- what don't you do, LOL

Jade1654: Couldn't have my own children or I would have. Scientist need to work on that part!

Joygirl636: LOL- ur so funny. What a great sense of humor you have.

Jade1654: Secret fantasy- always wanted to be a stand up comedian! New definition of S and M.......He snores......She masturbates!

Joygirl636: LOL, good one will have to re-member that one. S and M, LOL

Jade1654: well I have kept you long enough. I don't see how you work with no more sleep than you get.

Joygirl636: What do you mean?

Jade1654: I saw one of Tom's old cell bills on his phone. I don't see how either one of you were very productive at anything other than being on the phone. One cell bill of his was $800.

Joygirl636: well take care…I really enjoyed our talk tonight.

Jade1654: Yeah, we didn't talk about HIM all the time!

CHAPTER 5

Trying to Survive

You may not agree, but I felt at the time, the way of finding out the truth was to jump right into the middle of this and make it a threesome. Hey, three's a crowd as the old saying goes and he being MY husband- she was the one to go as far as I was concerned.

And there was the other motive. I admit it. If I moved back into his house, it would take a nuclear bomb to get me to leave this time! For all the pain and suffering I had gone through the previous six months- his ass was going to pay.

Tom had the next two nights off. We agreed we would talk about the situation with Joygirl. I couldn't call her by her supposed real name, Jennifer, as it was mine and my daughter's first name.

I pulled out the items she had given him- the pictures, clothes and the cards.

I guess my woman's intuition kicked in or perhaps I really do make a good detective. But while we were looking at the pictures, it just didn't add up.

I asked him again how old she claimed to be. He got a little angry but he replied with, *"twenty one and will be twenty two on July 8th"*.

Firing back, I told him he could get pissed off if he wanted to but I asked him nicely to look closely at one of the pictures-take a good, hard look Tom. This one you say is the most recent, according to her. If she is twenty one and it is the year 2003, please tell me when is the last time you have seen a twenty one year old wear a guy's class ring on her finger? Tom, they don't do that stuff anymore. Why is she wearing clothes and a hairdo that have been outdated for over twenty years? Tom, look at the sheets on the bed she is sitting on- avocado and harvest gold striped sheets? Come on- didn't ANY of that seem a little odd?

Of course not, he was happy. After all the time he has spent on the internet with her; the expensive hour-long phone calls; he was finally able to connect a face-even if it was just a picture- a quite so obvious picture to everyone BUT Tom that it was quite old.

How could he mistrust someone who poured her heart and soul to him in their hours of conversation? He knew her. She was the most loving, understanding and most trustworthy person he had ever met.

Trying to rationalize with him, I asked, *"How can you say that when you have never actually met her face to face? With the two of you living three states apart and the possibility of never meeting-she could be telling you anything-everything you WANT to hear."*

When I asked him what they talked about hours, numerous times during the day and night, he stated, *"Not as much about anything and sometimes about nothing at all."*

Inside, I was boiling mad as there were times about business issues or my doctor visits he would tell me it was not a good time or his voice mail picked up immediately. If I asked why his personal line was always busy he said he was on the internet or he was just busy. Not too busy to just sit and listen to her breathe!

I asked him to look at her handwriting. Maybe I have been around too many older people but I recognized the stroke and the characteristics of older penmanship. He told me I had a vivid imagination.

I asked him what gifts he had given her.

"She only wanted ten dollars," he replied.

But that wasn't what I asked him. So, I asked him again.

"Remember when you went with me and the boys to Bethlehem, NC and watched the lighting of the star for Christmas? There was a snow globe you admired at the store across the street when we were picking one out for Justin's girlfriend. The one you liked had bears on it."

Thinking back, I remembered a globe that had the cutest little teddy bears sitting on Christmas boxes and I had hoped that he would catch the hint and get it for me for Christmas.

He sent it to her instead. But she claimed that when she was taking it to show the other nurses, she accidentally left it in the car and as cold as it got through the night- it froze and it burst.

"Anything else?" I asked.

"I found a wholesaler who carried the perfume I bought overseas-you know Ciao-the one I bought for Beth when we were married and she didn't like it and left it under the lavatory sink-you know the one you liked so much?"

I remembered him telling me he found a wholesaler. But when I hinted I would love to buy some of it, he told me it was too expensive-evidently not expensive enough! Yep, you guessed it- he sent it to her!

Sorry, this is where I have to stop and take a blood pressure pill to continue writing...

Now I am talking about a man WHO in fours years of marriage HAD NOT given me so much as a card for my birthday (even though we had the same birthday so he couldn't have forgotten), our anniversary or any other sentimental day and he shipped a $140 an ounce bottle of perfume over three states to a supposed twenty one year old woman he had never met?

I felt completely devastated and numb. Yes, I hear you yelling - Run Forest Run!

I asked him how he could spend money and do such nice things for a complete stranger when he never did anything for me in five years. His answer was, *"She made him realize how insensitive he had been in the past and she demanded and asked for nice things. She brought out the best in him."*

OK on the count of three let's all puke! At that point, I had to question how many other men she had manipulated the very same way.

My comical side envisioned this woman walking down an aisle after aisle of a gigantic warehouse admiring her inventory of gifts from "suckers anonymous." What a player!

Jennifer Jade Benfield

But I must hand her the best actress award for pulling off this charade for over two years and not slipping up- until now........I am in the picture and slowly but surely she is talking to me more and more. And guess who is taking notes!!

For most women, curiosity kills the cat and I wasn't about to let this one rest until I was completely satisfied with all the facts.

Tom fell asleep early. I couldn't resist the temptation to find a phone number to contact this woman. I quietly sneaked into his day planner and yeppers- under the D's was a phone number- a cell number. Apparently, it was the only number she had ever given him.....imagine that.

I quickly memorized the number and returned the planner to his pants pocket, just like I found it. I grabbed my cell phone, a pack of cigarettes and headed out the door. After a few smokes, I got up the courage to dial the number.

When she answered, I asked for Jennifer. "*This is her,*" she answered. I was absolutely flabbergasted at the sound of her voice. A voice I will NEVER forget.

I sat quietly a few seconds collecting my thoughts from the shock. She said, "*This must be Jade as your number showed up on my caller ID.*"

Both of us remained cordial during the conversation but you could detect the hostility in our voices.

I first questioned why she continued contact with Tom when she found out he was married. She said she couldn't help herself. By the time she said she figured out he was still married; she was too involved to stop.

I explained I would appreciate it if she would stop having any contact at all with him as there were six lives at stake in the marriage between Tom and I and only one of her. But to no avail.

With a very hateful voice, she explained she would not go out with him until after he was divorced but she wasn't going to stop talking to him. Well you can imagine where the phone call went-down the toilet.

She got pissed and hung up on me.

At least now I knew what her voice sounded like, what her true intentions were and what pushed HER buttons. I'm gonna have fun with this BITCH if she continues to harass us.

The following night Tom was off. After he came in from his farm chores, I took a hot shower, put on some soothing body lotion, touched up my makeup and looked into those baby blue eyes of his with the look of – love me and take me now...I had never felt closer to him than that moment.

He looked directly into my eyes with tears streaming down his face. Just as I thought he was going to tell me he loved me, he softly said, "*I miss her.*"

Most women would have packed and left that night right then but as hurt as I was; I knew if I left I would have never gotten the information I needed for my divorce attorney. We needed to know the real identity of this woman and all the information I can dig up about this "affair" her and Tom were having. So through the roughest emotions I have ever felt, I asked him what was missing. All he could say was that he missed her.

The next day, his youngest son Daniel had a ballgame. We agreed to put up a good front for his sake and go to the game together. During the second inning, the oldest son asked where his dad was. I explained he said he was going to the bathroom but 30 minutes had passed so I left out to look for him. Found him alright- propped up against the fence talking to her. He had no clue I was anywhere around. He was explaining he had better return to the game before anyone noticed he was missing when I jumped around in front of him and said, "Too late."

I blasted both of them for being so damn selfish and stupid. I called her a bitch for putting herself before his son's ballgame. And I ripped him for not being able to tear himself away for an hour ballgame and his son should come first. I wanted to take his cell phone and slam it against the block building but that would have caused a scene so I opted to go sit back down. By the time he returned, the game was in the last inning and he had missed his son's championship ballgame.

Needless to say, the ride home was quiet and very strained. I went to bed crying my eyes out with Tom right behind me. He knew he was in trouble and he needed to fix things. I was crying so uncontrollably, I asked him to take the boys to his mothers. He obliged.

I was still out of control when he returned.

"How can you do such a thing? How can you treat your kids, my kids, your wife, OUR family this way over someone you have never met? After all we have been through in the past, how can you do this?"

The truth finally came out.

He said he was in love with her and he could not control himself or explain it. He told me when he learned I knew of the two of them, he had to do something to protect her. He did not want me to involve her in our divorce so the only thing he could think of was to move me back into his trailer. He couldn't explain what it was about her but he felt he had no worries when he talked to her. He felt he could be having the toughest of days and her child-like giggle washed away all his worries.

"In all these hours of conversation Tom, do you ever speak of the normal life- the real world?"

"Such as?"

"Well let's try the amount of income it takes to pay the house payment, groceries, cars and insurance, and the $600 a month child support that gets paid before we pay anything else. Does she realize how much strain it puts on a marriage to meet that obligation? And what about herself? I was screaming to the top of my lungs.

"What do you mean?"

"Supposedly being sooooo young"

He interrupts me with, *"She said she would settle for ten good years with me!"*

"That's not what I was talking about. How will you handle her eventually wanting children ten or less years down the road? You barely find time for your own two much less than a second family."

"Ten years of happiness. I will settle for ten years and just see what happens."

"I loved you unconditionally for all these years and I just can't believe you would fall for something as bizarre as this mystery woman. Have you given

any thought that you may be having a mid-life crisis and the fantasy of such a younger woman excites you?"

"That's the most ridiculous thing I have ever heard of!"

"Tom, I have an appointment with Dr. Betty tomorrow- will you please come with me?"

Now did you notice he NEVER answered the question about dealing with the "real world?"

I'm not going to spend a lot of time on the therapist session as you know what his answer was every time she tried to rationalize with him. His constant answer was, *"She doesn't know what she's talking about."*

He told Dr. Betty that he loved me and I told him that was an all out lie. He denied having an affair with anyone. He wasn't having a mid-life crisis of any kind and he was through with the session. Outside, he screamed at me for wasting his time and $115.00 of insurance money because that woman was crazy. He told me the reason he denied everything was to keep one less person off the witness stand for if he answered her questions, he would have admitted to something that would cost him later in court and I wasn't getting a penny. I could drop dead first.

We fought for days. His every waking moment

was spent trying to sneak a way to talk to Joygirl. Every breath spoken to me was asking for a divorce. The more he asked; the more stubborn I became.

He was catching it from both sides as Joygirl was pressuring him to get a divorce and I sure as hell wasn't going to give him one or move out.

Joygirl and I fought on the phone. Then there were days we would talk without incident. She trying to figure me out or play mind games and I was mostly taking notes. I took notes on every little detail her or Tom said. Then when he was gone, I pulled them out and put them in some kind of order that made chronological sense.

Pouring over my notes, nothing made sense. She spoke of a much older brother- one week he was fifty one and the next week he was fifty. When I asked her the age of her mother, she told me she was fifty four. Hmmmmmmmm..........That would be medical history. Even if she screwed up the age of her mother and let's say she did have a brother in his fifties-that would make her mother having her- well you do the math. Not entirely impossible but just makes the story that much more ridiculous.

One day she asked about Tom's and my sex life. I told her that was personal but before she came into our lives, it was very good.

OK, let's see where this is going.

She proceeded to tell me she wasn't very experienced in sex. Her roommate, Edie and her friends, Taffy, Laura and Jami said she wouldn't get so grouchy if she got laid. My only remark was, *"perhaps not."*

You could tell she got irritated because I didn't respond perhaps as long as she wanted.

She said she was not very experienced in sex having only had sex on the hood and backseat of a car once. I still had no remark.

Now comes the button pusher.....

She told me of a "sexual show" she watches of Dr. Johanson's on cable.

"Know of it, but never watch it." I said rather nonchalantly.

She said she was watching it one night while talking to Tom. She told him of a bullet vibrator she bought during one of those "girlie parties." She asked him how to use it. She explained that she really didn't know what to do with it other than rubbing it on her clit. So he told her how to do it. I am still not saying much.

At this point, I am just letting her babble away. He then told her to move it just below her clit before she had an orgasm to feel the outside of her

"G" spot. Then he told her to move it to the inside and tighten your muscles for the ultimate orgasm. She said she had moved into the kitchen so her roommate Edie wouldn't hear her and had such a hard orgasm that she nearly fell off the kitchen counter.

My only response was, *"And your point is?"*

"I enjoyed it so much, I thought you might want to try it", she quipped back.

"You silly woman! Who do you think taught him all about that?" I said laughing.

CLICK went the phone. Joygirl had a nasty habit of hanging up when she got angry or you told her something she didn't want to hear.

I just had to have the last word AND the last laugh from that day's conversation.

I didn't bother to ask Tom for details about the phone sex she described. There was plenty of time to do that when the time was right.

And she's not going to tell him the two of us talked because it will piss HIM off.

Hey! This is working out good for me. This mind game stuff is a lot of fun.

CHAPTER 6

Messing with Their Minds

Driving back from shooting pool late one Monday night, I decided to mess with her brain a bit and called her. WOW! No voice mail- she actually answered the phone so what was Tom doing?

Her topic for the evening was a doctor named Doug who had asked her out. He is also quite older but only in his early thirties, imagine that! Edie, her roommate works for him and has tried to convince her for months to go out with him. Edie says Joygirl needs to start seeing Dr. Doug" to get over her feelings with Tom.

The first thing said that actually has been the truth. She DOES need to get over MY HUSBAND.

I laughed to myself as I knew it was just another

"jerk wad scheme" to drive Tom into the loony house with jealousy and hopefully keep me off her trail.

"Details girl, give me details," I laughingly said; trying to muster up some excitement.

She told me he was a fine specimen of a man. He was 6' 4", slim and trim yet muscular, dark hair and a dark tan. OK- by now you should know me well enough I have already begun to dissect the description to pieces.

I asked myself, *"What magazine did she pick him out of?"* Muttering to myself, *"Bullshit!"* but at this point, I'm not responding back.

"You say something? Hello? Jade, are you there?" as she began to sound worried.

Gees did I really say that loud enough for her to hear me?

*"Sorry yummy thoughts of the good doctor's physique were racing through my brain. Dark tanned **and** muscular- good combination and sooooo nothing like Tom,"* I said.

"What do you mean?"

"Well, Tom is tall and trim but the boy is white as a ghost, has chicken legs and certainly is not muscular! Not to mention, you just described my third husband Rodger. I find it more than just ironic that your dating situation is so paralleled to my

marriages. I am usually attracted to dark haired, tanned men and ended up marrying Tom. You were interested in Tom and now seeing someone totally opposite. Guess it wouldn't be too obvious to Tom for you to date someone so totally opposite the spectrum to get his attention or ....would it?"

Suddenly, there was dead silence.

What? No comeback from the comeback kid from Missouri?

CLICK......There she goes again. Guess she didn't like what I had to say.

Just as I was pulling in the long drive to our trailer, my cell phone rang. I thought it might be Tom wondering what was taking me so long but it was Joygirl.

"I thought you got mad at me and hung up."

"Well, (a long pause) *I did get mad and I did hang up but I realized I hadn't told you of my and Doug's dating plan."*

I thought to myself. Damn, she is really deter-mined to entertain me tonight.

"He is taking me to my niece's ballgame and then we're getting ice cream afterwards."

"Don't forget the sugar-free!"

"Sugar- free?"

"Well, you don't need the sugar rush- you being diabetic and all."

"Oh yeah, right.....Well I will let you know how the date goes ok?

Before I had the chance to answer- CLICK; she hung up.

Heads----I tell.

Tails----I don't.

Hee! Hee! Tails it is. Is this a very rational way of dealing with such a complicated and miserable marriage? Maybe not, but it is my way.

When I coasted in the driveway to the end of the trailer, I could see Tom's bedroom light on. No doubt he is talking to Joygirl, hence the reason for her hanging up on me so abruptly. I deliberately slam the car door a little harder than usual so he can hear that I am home. The bedroom light suddenly goes out. At this point, I think I want to have a little fun. So, instead of coming in the house right away, causing them to hang up, I quietly sat down on the back deck and smoked a cigarette or two. I call Joygirl's cell and it goes straight to voicemail. When someone calls on her line while she is talking with someone else, you can most definitely hear the silent pause that someone is beeping in. If she answered it, she would have to tell Tom she had to answer the other line, then, tell him a lie about who it was. If she ignored it, then he will want to know why she didn't answer her phone.

Oh, I do love this mind game stuff. No wonder people get addicted to jerking someone's chain-they have no life and all this drama.

I called Tom's cell and left a message that I was on the back deck enjoying a cigarette while he talked to his precious Joygirl. Suddenly, you could hear hard footsteps coming down through the trailer. He opens the back door with such force that it threw the chain off the frame. As I took a drag off the cigarette, I calmly looked back at him and asked if anything was wrong. He just looked at me and stomped back to his bedroom.

A few days passed and while cordially watching television together, Tom got up the nerve to ask if I had heard from Joygirl. It appears her scheme for me to tell about "Dr. Doug" has derailed. The snag being........I didn't tell Tom.....OOPS

Oh boy, did I push a button this time.

With laptop in place, he is pecking away and he appears furious.

"But loving me the way she did........" *"What does she mean by DID?"*

He is asking me this? Did I just hear what I think I heard?

"Well we are still married and we are still living under the same roof as husband and wife; I guess she .... (I paused to throw some more drama

in) *has given up on your relationship. From what I got out of the conversation with her a couple of days ago, he is good looking, tanned and rich......but a <u>slut puppy</u>.*" I threw that in too for drama to push his button.

"YOU ARE THE CAUSE OF ALL OF THIS!" shouting so loud his face turned beet red. *"IF YOU WOULD JUST GIVE ME A DIVORCE; I COULD BE HAPPY."*

"Not a chance Sparky...Only way you will get rid of me out of this dump is in a pine box." I said it laughing so hard my side hurt.

He got on the laptop pounding away at the keys. She obviously didn't answer any of his messages. For hours, he just sat there glaring at the screen, fuming more and more as time passed. And, he knew better than to call her with me around. When I last looked at the clock, it was 4 am and he was boiling like a volcano- waiting for a response that I knew was never going to come.

CHAPTER 7
And the BS Flies

Joygirl636: wanna play spades?

Jade1654: sure

Joygirl636: after the ballgame and ice cream he took me swimming. i love to swim. he told me not to quit my day job.

Jade1654: how's that and who are you talking about?

Joygirl636: i was singing to him at the pool. i always thought i sang good at the pool- sounded good to me! i am talking about doug- dr doug

Joygirl636: doug says hello

Jade1654: Well you can tell him you won't quit your night job and ur singing will be just fine

Joygirl636: he just walked in and wants to learn spades

Jade1654: Didn't take you two long to get real chummy real fast after one date.

Damn, if the slack-ass phone company would ever update the prehistoric phone system we have here; I could have DSL and call her bluff about the good doctor.

I picked up my cell phone to call her cell but my battery was dead. I forgot to charge my battery------damn.

She is dead wrong if she thinks I am going to play into her hands.

Jade1654: Tell him I said good luck and let's kick some ass.

The rest of the night I played spades with her but didn't say much to her. I was too busy messaging Rita back and forth scheming up mind games. I told Rita I would call her after Joygirl called.

Sure enough like clockwork, the phone rang.

In an almost-possessed tone of voice she quirked off, *"Why did you blow me off?"*

"What the hell are you talking about?" I asked trying to keep a straight face.

"You blew me and Doug off while we were play-ing spades and I want to know why?

"I thought you wanted to play spades and teach the good doctor how to win. That is a little hard to do chatting back and forth like a bunch of school

girls—so I was trying hard to win."

"Well you could have at least chatted with us some while we played. I figured you would have some questions for Doug since he was sitting right here."

"I really had nothing to ask him since I am not the one going out with him- you are and to tell the truth, I had a hard enough time trying to play spades and talk to Tom at the same time. Three things going on at once gets a little difficult at times, you know?"

"Talking to Tom," she interrupted. At this point, I wondered if her head was spinning around like Linda Blair's in the Exorcist.

CLICK...........Pissed again. I know she was most likely calling him at work, giving him hell for talking to me so long. Wonder if she was using that same tone of voice with Tom she used on me.

"Hey Rita"

"What girlfriend?"

"High five babe as we pushed some major buttons!"

"Mad was she?"

*"She was so pissed she sounded like the **bitch from hell**....Certainly not all giggly and naive. I bet he is really catching it now. I can hear him now......*

"I'm not lying. I really haven't talked to her

since I left the house at 9 this morning."

"I bet the more he denies, the angrier she gets" I said with delight.

Rita and I laughed so hard we could barely contain ourselves.

"Wait Rita, there is a message on the screen."

Joygirl636: Tell Tom not to contact me anymore. I have become a liar and a cheat just like him and I don't like it. Have a nice life!

"When did she send that?"

"I don't know-since I was talking to you. I had messenger up and then closed it."

As I finished my conversation with Rita, Tom was coming through he door from the saw mill.

"Come over here a minute Tom. I need you to read something" as I pointed to the laptop screen.

"When did she send that?"

"I don't know. I just turned on the computer to send Mary a note about some one in our graduating class passing away and there was the offline message."

"Offline messages...she hates those things. Why did she send it that way?"

"I don't know Tom. I figured it was just another jerk wad scheme or something you two plotted together to throw me off track.

Slam went the door after he shot me a look that

could kill and back stomping to the saw mill he went.

Let's analyze this....

1. If she really wanted to break it off with Tom, she would have sent the message to his ID(s). See I included multiples because at this point he thinks he has pulled off a "slick Rick" on me by using other ids. But I know both of their ids. What he doesn't know is that I had become more computer literate while we were separated so now there are no more secrets!

2. If she really wanted to break it off, she would call him; then she would have killed the screen IDS and terminated her cell phone service or changed her number so he couldn't contact her.

3. If she was really breaking it off with Tom, he would have reacted more violently, been pissed and tried to contact her. He simply slammed the door upon hearing my accusation and went back to work.

CHAPTER 8
The Breakdown

A few days later, I emerged from the home office to find Tom rocking back and forth on the couch, tightly holding a pillow. He is crying uncontrollably as I had done for months before.

"Tom, Tom......Tooooommmmmmm" nearly screaming to the top of my lungs. He isn't even aware I am in the room as I sat down beside of him.

I asked myself- is he having a nervous breakdown or has she actually broken it off with him?

He collapsed in my lap. The tears pouring down his face; his nose dripping and slobber coming out of his mouth. I have never witnessed him cry this way. For two hours we sat- not a word to each other- just his uncontrollable wailing.

Feeling sorry for his pitiful look, I got up and

wet a washcloth. I wiped his face and as I caressed his head he blurted out, "*I have nothing left to give you. I can't do this anymore.*"

"*But Tom, I have asked nothing of you but your love- that is all I have asked of you since I met you. You have put yourself in this terrible predicament. Why Tom? Why this infatuation with a woman you have never met. Why this woman you have shared your deepest, darkest secrets, your fantasies, your hopes, your dreams-everything you should be shar-ing with me, <u>your wife</u>, not some stranger. You are completely out of character. I am worried about you.*"

"*We were having so many troubles. The busi-nesses, work, your illness- I just couldn't take it any more. Talking to her on the internet was an escape at first. Then she gave me her phone number and we would just talk for hours. She was a good listener. Then one night I called her. It was back the first of December, maybe late November; but she was play-ing bingo with her mom and friends at some local lodge. It was a coverall game and she only needed two numbers. Next thing you know she blurts out BINGO and in the same breath she told me she loved me. It was the raspy giggle- you know the one when she is excited. Her telling me she loved me-SHE LOVED ME! And, at a time in my life when I needed someone to tell me they loved me......THEY LOVED ME...*

"But baby....I told you I loved and adored you. You were my life."

"There was so much baggage in our marriage it wasn't fun any more."

"FUN????? Yeah, I know Tom. It's called life."

"While talking to her on the phone or chatting online- it was so carefree, no worries- just fun. Well, unless she pouted or I pissed her off and she would hang up. We would talk and laugh and she made me feel wanted. I know I love her, no matter what you say. And, I am going to be with her despite what you or anyone else thinks. Despite everything and every one."

"But Tom don't you realize that if you move out there or she here that it will be the real world facing you, the same problems we have to deal with of bills, house payment, child support to pay? You're just running away from problems that can be resolved between us."

"But Joygirl says that everything will be alright as soon as we are together no matter where we live."

OH MY GOD, how has she managed to brainwash this guy into thinking there is no real world out there to contend with every day?

CHAPTER 9

The First Trip

The remainder of the week passed by quickly without much incident- he at one end of the house and me at the other. It was obvious he had not spoken to her. He was irritable, nervous and absolutely no fun to be around at all.

He had tried to pick a fight with me all morning. I calmly sat reading the Sunday paper and drinking coffee, my usual Sunday ritual to unwind from the prior week's torture.

"It's your fault you know, if you would just give me a divorce. It is her I love, I want, not yours. It is her I want to make love to, not you."

"Then go to her. But I am never leaving this house ever again. I told you that. And if you leave, you better not ever come back here with her. If you

want the divorce so badly, then you can move and you can pay for the divorce. Last year, I presented you with three sets of separation papers and you refused to sign. Now months later, I am stuck in this hellhole with NOTHING. The only home my kids have ever grown up in has been foreclosed, my furniture is gone- hell I don't even have a car, checking or savings account in my own name anymore. You have cut off everything and I am still here."

He just sat there stunned.

"I have jumped through hoops for you; put up with your spoiled ass brat tantrums; you talking down to me and your family treating me like a redheaded stepchild. I am making my stand, right here, right now!"

"I have never hit a woman," as he came at me with his fist balled up.

"Take your best shot as it will be your last and you will never meet your precious Joygirl."

He stomped off to the master bedroom. You could hear him throwing things around. He emerged with his golf clubs, cue case and clothes bag in hand.

"I'm leaving for a few days to clear my head."

"How stupid do you think I am Tom? I know exactly where you are going and it's not Myrtle Beach. So why take all that stuff?"

"I don't know where I'm going. I've just got to get away."

"She won't see you!"

"She loves me; of course she will see me."

"Oh, you naive, pathetic man- you'll never get to meet her. She'll never meet you because she would have to admit she lied to you about who she really is."

"You're the one who's lying. You'll see. You're just saying these things to break us up."

"In the end, you will see who is telling the truth. See you later," as I slammed the door behind him and locked it.

"Maybe you will be gone if and when I come back."

"Oh hell no, that would be too damn easy and convenient for you. What are you going to do about work? You're supposed to go tonight for your three on night shift."

"F--- work! I'll leave Page a message later that I am taking a few days off."

"But you don't have any time left to take off with pay. You used them already."

Out the drive he went with a trail of dust behind him. He didn't care the house payment was due; if there were groceries; or if I had any money. With the checking account and the house payment in his name, all I could do was hope that he would be back in a day or two.

He no sooner turned out the drive, the phone rang.

"Where's Tom?"

"Hi pop" trying to think of something quickly. *"He's already left for work."*

"It's only one in the afternoon. Why did he leave so early?"

The only answer I could think of was, *"I guess something came up work."*

"Get him to call me tomorrow when he gets in from work in the morning."

"Anything I can do for you pop?"

"Well.....I wanted him to check the cows for more calves. I'll talk to him later bye."

Bob was notorious for asking for Tom when a simple message would suffice. Always the same conversation- having to drag stuff out of him or finding out through Tom leaving a message with me would have been just as productive. That man never gave me any credit to know how to "get out of the rain." The *city girl* he had called me when I first met him.

I made up my mind when I hung up that if Tom wasn't back the next day, I was going to tell his parents where he had gone. No more covering for him.

Guess I had better call Rita with the update and the daily "ass chewing" for putting up with this mess.

"Stop laughing, damn it! Cut it out and let me explain it all."

"Oh Jade, you know I am not laughing at you. I am laughing at the dumb ass speeding West on I-40 and he has a hell-of-a-drive ahead of him. We both know she won't see him when he gets there."

"I have told him a hundred times, but he knows this girl, remember?"

I started laughing hysterically. Now we are both laughing. I laughed so hard I wet my pants. Damn it's hell getting older. Well I guess this young girl won't have to worry about depends for quite a few years!

"Least we can do is look after each other considering the pricks we are both married to," Rita reminded me.

I no sooner hung up the phone when it rang again. I nearly jumped out of my skin it startled me so badly.

"I am on my way to Missouri."

"I already know that Tom. It took me all of a second to know where the hell you were going. I have been with you since Oct. 13, 1998. I know you better than you know yourself. And I know you must

take this trip to get this infatuation out of your head for good. When you find out she is not who she pretends to be, drive on home. I am upset and deeply hurt but I know this has to be done."

I didn't wait for a response. I just hung up.

At nearly dusk, the phone rang again.

"I am still on the road."

"Have you talked to her yet?"

"Yeah, she said she won't see me and for me to turn around and go back to North Carolina. But I'm gonna see her. I'm gonna drive to Cape Girardeau and sleep a while. I will be there soon."

"So do you think you will be able to find her?"

"Don't you think it is a little odd that you have tried to contact her for days and suddenly she is answering her phone?"

"Well she did say she thought it was someone else."

"And you fell for that Tom? Did you forget she has caller ID on her phone?"

"Well......yeah."

"Well......duh!"

"I guess she finally answered it because I have called so much. Jade did you call her and tell her I was coming? Man, I wished you hadn't. She said she wouldn't see me until I was divorced. DAMN IT.....DID YOU CALL HER?"

"Before you get your panties in a wad, NO, I didn't call her. I am staying out of this to let her explain all the lies and deceit she has pulled over on you and let you get your mind back to reality. I am confident she is not going to meet you and I will prove to you before you get back she is not who she says she is. **I will prove I am not lying to you-she is!**"

"Oh, by the way Tom, your Dad called just after you left today. I covered for you today but when he calls tomorrow, I am not covering for you any longer. I am going over to the house and explain it all-lay it all out on the table- the BS I have put up with all these months."

Well now he has taken up the habit of Joygirl as he has hung up on me just the way she does when things don't go her way.

Monday evening and Bob calls again.

"I will be right over pop. I need to talk to you and Lacy."

He could tell there was something wrong.

"I realize we have not gotten along well in the past but I still have respect for you and Lacy because you are Tom's parents. Bob, I lied to you about Tom's whereabouts yesterday and I am sorry. I don't lie to my parents and I am not going to lie to you now. Tom left yesterday for Missouri to locate

the twenty one year old he has been involved with from the internet. It is the same one who sends cards, letters and boxes to your address when she sends it."

They were furious and appalled that he could do such a thing-something so stupid and with good reason to be furious.

Tom was walking away from a very good paying job (a job he held for nearly ten years). He has responsibilities on the farm as his father's health was failing. Both his parents had spent quite a bit of money on Tom the past few years (passed it out like Halloween candy was more like it). And, Bob had spent thousands of dollars for Tom to build a saw mill to help supplement Tom's income to pay his expensive child support.

"I found in his bedroom an application with the postal service in Memphis and St. Louis. It appears he is planning on moving out there to be closer to her" I said crying.

"He is willing to walk away from all his responsibilities here to be with her?" his mom said with her mouth gapped open.

I had been telling them for quite some time Tom stayed on the computer way too much. They felt it was all in my imagination.

After we separated, Tom moved in with his parents and they got to see firsthand how much time he spent on the computer.

Bob expressed how disappointed he was that he wasn't taking care of the cows as he should and things weren't getting done around the farm. If he mentioned it to Tom, Tom got mad and would storm out of the house.

I asked Lacy how much the cell phone bill had been running the past few months. Her only comment was, "*Way over the minutes. In fact, he has been on the phone so much, it has been cutting into the minutes of mine and Bob's phone and still owing money.*"

You only imagine the pain and disgust I felt knowing that Tom was still having extreme contact with Joygirl even though he and I were back together. Of course, she is going to cover for her "precious little boy". From what Bob said, "The apple doesn't fall far from the tree as he married Lacy not knowing who the father of Tom really was either."

So anything Tom does, she won't betray him. So, in my eyes, she condoned everything he has done. Like mama, like son. What's good for one, fair for the other, right?

I was pretty pissed covering for him that first night but what could I do?

When I gave Tom's explanation for moving me

back in; they were furious and embarrassed. For once in five years, we were close to being on the same page. They saw I wasn't the villainess they thought me to be or as Tom had convinced them I was.

"I have to go. I'm sorry. I just have to go." as the tears were streaming down my face.

"Do you need anything? Could you use some money?" Lacy asked as the tears weld up in her eyes.

"No, he left with all the money but I don't need anything. I will be alright. I have groceries and drinks. I will be alright. Bob, I will look after the cows for you and take a head count in the morning for new calves. I enjoy that anyway. Thank you for all your kindness."

I backed myself out the door with embarrassment.

"Don't hesitate to ask if you need anything. Will you let us know if you hear from him?" Bob sat looking up at me like a little puppy. I felt so sorry for him as he had done so much for Tom all these years.

"Sure." I answered as I had two things on my mind. I am sure they blame me for everything that is going on as they have never liked me from day one. That "city girl" they always called me. They

wouldn't give me the time of day if it didn't have to do with Tom.

When I got home, I just collapsed on the front porch crying uncontrollably. I looked up at the stars. They were so bright and the sky so clear, I just wanted to reach up and touch them.

"Oh God, please help Tom and watch over him while he is out there. Help him find the strength to see through this woman for whom and what she is. Please God help me find the information on this woman to prove who she really is before it is too late for us all..."

I sat in a lawn chair on the front porch for most of the night. Nightmares reoccurred when I tried to sleep. My mind raced 24/7. As the light of dawn appeared, the phone rang.

"I'm ok. I'm just exhausted. You ok?"

"I haven't slept."

"You should have slept."

"And just how do you think I could sleep with my husband running all over the country looking for someone he has never met, doesn't really know what she looks like or if she has thugs out waiting for you? Have you been able to figure out where she lives?"

"No, but I am going to get a room with internet and rest some. I will start back at Cape Girardeau

and get back at it in a few hours."

This man was driven like no other I had met before. If he had put a tenth of the passion into our marriage that he had done trying to find her, we wouldn't have had many problems.

Just as I started to ask him a question about the payment, there was dead silence. He had hung up on me. Now this is becoming a nasty, rude habit.

The day seemed to go by slowly. Both my children called and I tried to act "normal."

Rita and I must have spoken a half-dozen times that morning.

"Damn sorry Rita. I need to call the phone company and get a cheaper long distance plan. I will call you with an update when I get one."

"No Bob, I haven't heard anything from Tom and I haven't had a chance to get a head count on claves. I am out the door now to get one."

"No Lacy, I haven't heard anything from Tom. Bob just called asking the same thing; but, I guess you are at work. I will call you on your cell if I hear anything."

That afternoon Lacy came by the house in the truck. As I climbed into the truck, I know I must have looked like I was blindsided by a train by the look Lacy gave me.

"You sure you're ok?"

"I haven't slept much. Just naps on the porch when I drift off to sleep. He hasn't found her the last time I spoke with him. He is in Cape Girardeau."

"How could he pull such a ridiculous stunt?"

"I don't know Lacy. He's your son. You raised him with your values. You tell me how he could pull such a stunt. You're his mother. You're supposed to know him better than anyone. He is just completely infatuated. Men in middle age life crisis do stupid things."

"Middle age WHAT?"

"You know- the "40 thang" They reach that age between 35 and 40-something and they think life has gone to hell in a hand basket. She obviously is telling him all the things he needs to hear from someone other than me to stroke his ego and he is eating it up like cotton candy at the county fair."

"Look....a new baby calf. That makes nine," Lacy squealed with delight.

"He has all this beauty around him. You and Bob have practically handed him anything he wanted through life and he appreciates nothing. How can he throw all of it away for some mindless twit three states away that he has never met?"

"I don't know. I simply just do not know but I

need to get back to Bob and fix supper. Want to join us?"

"I appreciate the invite but I don't have much of an appetite, thanks anyway."

I knew under that hardened exterior there was a human being in there somewhere; but in five years, I had never witnessed it.....until today. Today, we actually shared something together- disappointment in the man we both loved.

The phone was ringing when I walked into the house.

"She stood me up...She stood me up." Tom was screaming and crying at the same time.

"Slow down Tom. Catch you breath. Are you parked somewhere?"

"She agreed to meet with me and she stood me up."

Part of me wanted to say I told you so and burst out laughing. But I knew it took a lot of trust for him to call me and confess.

"Ok, talk slowly. Catch your breath and go through the whole afternoon with me and let me see if I can figure any of this out."

"I called her this morning. She originally told me she couldn't meet me because she had a class at the hospital and she couldn't get out of it."

"What kind of class Tom? If she recently gradu-

ated, you would think she should have taken all the required classes and if there were some sort of clinicals, I don't think she could have gotten out of that so easily."

"I don't know. You would think so. Maybe it is some sort of orientation class or something," he snapped back.

"Calm down Tom. I'm just trying to help you think things through. Please don't snap at me. But you sound like you doubt her. Quite frankly, I have doubted this person since the first time I spoke to her on the phone. Anyway, what did she have to say?"

"She told me to drive to Bonne Terre to a Super 8 hotel there. Across the street was a Huddle House. She told me to go check in and she would try to get out of class."

"Sounds like she knows the area."

"Everything was just as she described."

"Right down to the dummy that drove there," I mumbled. *"If you were close enough to the general area where she lived, why didn't she give you her house phone number to call or the hospital number when you got there?"*

"She said she wanted to keep the line open in case the meeting was cancelled and she also had a bad experience once with a guy from the internet

that she gave her phone number to. It is quite a bizarre story from what she told me. You should get her to tell you the story sometime."

Again, I mumbled, *"Nearly as bizarre as this one!"*

"Anyway I drove to Bonne Terre and got settled in and called her back."

"What do you mean you got settled in?" As if I didn't know..."If you just wanted to meet her for coffee why in the hell are you renting a motel room BEFORE you meet her?"

You could tell he was getting as pissed as I was.

"While talking with her on her cell, her house phone rang. It was her instructor from the hospital."

How convenient to "stage" the whole thing over the phone while she had him on the other line. She probably had a friend call her on her house phone to stage the whole thing. But you know how God made men....they can only carry blood to one head or the other but not both!

"Why set up a time to meet me only to stand me up in the end-making me pay for a motel room and all. I waited so long at the Huddle House I thought they were going to have me arrested and her brother being a cop and all I was afraid they thought I was a stalker."

While I am quietly laughing and enjoying a cigarette, I have these visions of a guy with North Carolina plates just going around in circles all over the block; looking for a car that doesn't exist; looking for a woman he has no clue what she looks like; looking for a hospital he has no clue what the name of it is, thinking to myself- why do book smart people have no common sense and are so DAMN STUPID!

God has a sense of humor after all!

"She has no intention of meeting you in the first place silly. Are you sure you are at the right Huddle House?" Oh my God, I can't believe I am helping this man try to find her. Now I have lost MY mind.

"Yes, damn it" snapping at me.

"Now don't start snapping at me asshole. I am trying to help. That is a hell of a lot more than other wives would do."

"I'm sorry. I just haven't had a lot of sleep lately and I am getting frustrated. She described all these landmarks around the motel and the restaurant so I know I'm at the right one. She really did mean it when she said she wouldn't meet with me until I was divorced."

"Do you think maybe this is just a big joke that has been carried out way too far? Can you please

just come home and let's try to forget all of this; put it all behind us and start our marriage over?"

"HEY, I called you because I was worried sick about HER not hear insults from you! Now, there was a really bad storm here a couple of hours ago while I was waiting inside the Huddle House. Perhaps a tree blew over or she is trapped."

"She's trapped alright. She is caught up in her own lies and can't figure a way out of them. It wouldn't surprise me if she isn't sitting in her car right now watching you, laughing her ass off. It wouldn't surprise me if she isn't sitting directly across from you in another booth watching you right now."

"OK chill out. I need you to do something for me. Please call her cell phone to see if she will answer?"

"You want me to do WHAT? You're f------ kidding me, right?"

"Please, please. I am worried sick. You two seem to have hit it off. Maybe she will talk to you and you can convince her to talk to me."

Gee, he is soooo clueless! We "hit it off" because it has been one mind game after another with me trying to stay two steps ahead of her. And I would like to hit it off with her alright- knock her block off with a good right hook!

"What are you going to do in the meantime?"

You could tell something was wrong by the tone of his voice. *"There are several cop cars positioned around and one just drove through the parking lot."*

"Are you inside or outside?"

"I'm in the car."

"Maybe they are suspicious and they called the law from the Huddle House. But, I will tell you this. If you didn't look like a pedophile, now would be the perfect time to expose this woman. Take the Christmas cards and the letters to the police telling them this woman has been in contact with you as late as today and stood you up and you need to know if it is a hoax."

Slam went the phone. I guess he didn't like that answer either.

He called back stating that he had gone into the Huddle House to meet Jennifer Duncan but the waitress said she didn't know her.

"Tom, I have questions. If she had no plans to meet you, then why did you bother pursuing her; running all over the countryside like a little puppet? Why give her the satisfaction? And if all you wanted to do was meet for coffee then why get a motel room?"

CLICK...The truth hurts, huh? See, he forgets I am the one married to him and who knows him best.

I did try to call her several times but she wouldn't answer and I knew she wouldn't.

Tom was going berserk. She was playing him like a fiddle and I was three states away and four cartons of cigarettes later trying to console a low-down, cheating, near suicidal husband. Where's MY therapist when I need her?

We were up all night trying to find someone that didn't exist, I felt sure. But, there was no convincing him of that. I gave him information and directions to area hospitals. He drove around looking for any clues: the green Mustang she said she drove; an area hospital with multiple floors she described; the group home she claimed she worked part-time; apartment townhouses she said she lived at- nothing...Absolutely NOTHING.

Still none of this convinced him this whole life, this person he thought he was in love with was just a fabrication.

Very well planned and executed with one major snag.....I DIDN'T BELIEVE THE BITCH.

I know you are finally clapping with approval....but you knew I am smarter than what I appear, right? Right?

Several times we went back through the day trying to recall every detail. Perhaps he missed a hint in her conversation she was going to stand him up.

My mind kept pouring over facts to prove my case about this imposter- this extortionist....This sick person with her sick joke and her sick laughter.

My heart was also breaking as I felt if Tom had just put a third of this effort into our marriage; he wouldn't be running all over Missouri right now. We could be relaxing and laughing about old times like we used to and planning to make new memories. But Joygirl had stripped all joys of that away.

He must have tried to call her a hundred times. I dread our phone bill with all the long distance phone calls just to hear her damn voice mail with that deader than dead raspy voice.

"Tom, I can't get through to her. She won't answer the phone. Will you PLEASE give up this search and come back home?"

"I still want to find her."

"You're kidding right?"

"Hell no and somehow I will find her."

"I tried to make the house payment today but since my name isn't on the checking account I'm not authorized to transfer any money."

"I'll call Patty tomorrow. Give me the number to the bank."

"Tom, do you think her brother Steven may have called the cops on you today? You know she claims her brother would hurt you if you showed up."

"F--- him. I've got to see her. I didn't come all this way to be made a fool of."

"Sorry chump. But I am afraid that happened a long time ago when she first met you in the poker room."

"Guess I will go to the hotel and will stay in touch with you on Tuesday. And Jade, try to get some rest and thanks for trying to help me out."

Needless to say, I spent most of the second night in the chair on the porch looking up at the stars.

CHAPTER 10

Searching

"Rita, what cha doing?"

"Morning. He make it back home yet?"

"No, he's still out there riding around trying to find her. She still won't answer her cell. It is driving him nuts...and me too!"

"I had hoped he would have come to his senses by now but since he hasn't; it is time to use all our resources and stop all your anguish."

"Rita, what are you talking about?" She started describing all the surroundings of the area Tom was at.

"Rita, how do you know all those areas I have been talking about?"

"My mother grew up in Farmington and still has family there!"

"Oh my God, Rita. You are a God send. Pleeease help me. Jade you are the only reason I am doing this. As far as I am concerned, that jerk can stay gone for all he's put you through."

"You still don't understand why I am doing this, do you Rita?"

"Hell no. I think you're nuts!"

"When you think about it, didn't Mark go through the same thing just a little younger? Midlife crisis hits anywhere from thirty five to forty five. When Tom sees how foolish he has been; hopefully he will snap out of it."

"God, you're such an idiot!"

"Maybe so, but I'm an idiot still in love with the man I married and I won't give up on him just yet. Beside's Rita, think about it. If we do end up in divorce, it can only help my case to stick it out. Not to mention, I'm gonna ride this out whether we make it or not just to prove who this "Joygirl" person really is. I have never been more determined to prove something in my whole life. I have solved other mysteries before and I'm not giving up on this one. This is one person she can't fool. You in with me on this Rita? I promise you, it will be fun!"

"OK, what's your plan?"

"Thanks Rita. I love you for being here for me. First he gave me a list of hospitals in a sixty plus

mile area. I want to call all the HR departments of the hospitals to verify employment of a Jennifer Duncan. On my search so far, there isn't a Jennifer Duncan in her twenties in the whole state of Missouri.

Second, I've been searching through OB-GYNs in a sixty plus mile area for a doctor named Doug, Douglas or the letter D. She has obviously fabricated him also as there are no OBs with the first name of Doug or Douglas, not even a David. I have my suspicions about who she really is from the very start but I wanted to gather my facts first."

"OK, stay in touch. Email me if you run across anything. I'll work on the doctor list while you try to verify the employment."

"Oh Rita, I'm also checking real estate companies for townhouse rentals."

Most of the day was spent on the computer. I don't see how people maintain an eight hour day at those things five days a week. My neck was sore, my eyes were strained, my back was killing me and as I affectionately call it, "my big ole ass" was numb. At least when I worked on the computer in sales at CommScope, I could pace around my cubicle, which drove my associates nuts at times. Enough rambling though.

Now think of all the resources to track someone down:

1. Cities within a two hour drive to Ironton, Missouri.
2. Postal verification of those possible cities that used Cape Girardeau for mail routing.
3. Cell phone billing.
4. Car registration.
5. Driver license.
6. Doctors.
7. Hospitals.
8. Temp Services.
9. Real Estate Transfers.
10. Real Estate Rental Companies.
11. Real Estate and personal tax listings.
12. Block Buster video stores.
13. Wal Marts in the surrounding area.
14. Retail stores that specialize in nursing scrubs.
15. Group homes for the mentally challenged.

She claimed she worked third shift at one. She claimed she drove a van on Saturdays taking them places like McDonalds and such. One name stood out. She mentioned him often-Joey.

"WOW, you've been doing your homework but still no Jennifer Duncan?" Tom asked disappointingly.

"All leads point to a fabrication, sorry babe. So, when are you heading home?"

"I don't know. I have tried to call her but voice mail picks up."

"Did you go by the post office as I suggested?"

"Which post office? Do you know how many little towns are out here when you suggested that?"

"You're not thinking Tom. She sent you a Christmas card with a return address on it. The least you could do is go by that address and find out who really lives there. Unless, you really don't want to face the truth as to whom this person REALLY IS. That is the least you could do while I'm stuck here at home trying to help you.

It seems perfectly obvious to me that everything originates from her 'so called' mother's address in Ironton. If you really wanted the truth that would have been the first place you would have checked out."

"Oh hell no! Her mother isn't fond of me and I promised Joygirl I wouldn't get her involved. I will respect her wishes."

"Oh Tom you're such a dumb ass. Of course she is going to tell you that so you won't search there for the truth. Did you go by the DMV and check for car titles, the post office or the tax office?"

"NO" he snapped.

"Listen you little snot-nosed brat! Just what the hell have you been doing then? I've been at this *damn computer and have run through every possible lead. It's time you got off your dead ass and either get the truth about this mess or come the hell home. I'm beginning to get pretty pissed about this whole situation. This is the third day without any rest and I can't take much more and neither can your parents. You're not even thinking about how your little escapade is affecting everyone else."*

"My parents?"

"I told you I wasn't going to cover for you. They are worried sick. You need to, at least, call them and reassure them you're not stepping off the deep end here."

"I'll talk to them when I come back home."

"And when will that be?"

"Tomorrow. Tomorrow. If I don't find anything out, I will leave tomorrow."

"There is one thing you need to do before you come home."

"What?"

"You need to suck it up, get some balls about you and go to Ironton to the return address and just find out who lives there. It can be done without actually going right up to the door. There are neighbors or wait for the mailman and ask them. Even if it is her REAL mom, what can she do- shoot you?"

My mind starts to drift. Oh, I don't think I could

be so lucky for someone to actually shoot him. At this point, I am so mad I could probably do it myself without blinking an eye.

"She could have me arrested!" he screamed.

"Tom, when you tell them the ridiculous fabrication of Joygirl, I think the law will just tell you to get the hell out of town and go back home where you should have been all along.

But if you would just go by the Ironton address and see what cars are parked outside, names on a mailbox, anything that would give us some clue then at least this mystery could be put to rest."

"I just can't disrespect her mom like that."

"OH MY GOD! Since when did you care about respecting someone else? Since when did what other people think or feel affect you? I think you are too scared to face the truth. Your fantasy is going to blow up soon- better to face the truth now."

CLICK...dead silence. What a nasty habit-hanging up on someone. Guess I'll eat something and try to make the best of the evening.

I must have dozed off before eating. I was so exhausted. I was sleeping deeply when the phone rang; it startled me so badly I thought I was having a heart attack.

"Where can I find a big arrangement of purple tulips?"

Jennifer Jade Benfield

"For what?"

"Joygirl's mom loves purple tulips and I thought I might go by there and leave Joygirl a note and try to explain to her mother I don't mean any harm. I just want to meet Joygirl. I thought I would get her several potted tulips and have them make her a huge arrangement as a peace offering."

"For starters, the huge arrangement would look like you are trying to buy her approval when a simple potted plant would be a more sincere gesture. Did you go by the post office to get directions to the address?"

"Yes, I even went by there but no one answered the door. It's a group of townhouse apartments or condos. The parking lot is sort of grown over and the buildings aren't maintained well."

"Joygirl said she lived in a townhouse with a roommate Edie, right?"

"Yes she did. What are you getting at?"

"Did you look for any Mustangs, particularly a green one?"

"How do you know what she drives? How did you know it was a green one? I didn't look for any particular car but I think I would have remembered a green one if I saw it. This town's not very big-about the size of the town you're from and a lot like it. The main highway runs down through the middle

of it and only one stop light."

"Gees Tom, as small as that town is then every-one knows each other. How hard can it be to stop in a convenience store and ask a few questions? Turn on that bullshit charm of yours. I am sure you can find out a lot if you would just try.

I'm glad you decided to contact her mother. Maybe now we can get some answers. Are you com-ing home soon?"

CLICK......You guessed it!

CHAPTER 11

The Showdown

"Jade, it's Rita. Did I wake you?"

"Yes, but it's ok. What time is it?"

"A little after 9am. It's good you got some sleep. Have you heard from him lately?"

"No, I blasted him late yesterday afternoon and told him to get off his dead ass and find out something or come home. He's gonna lose his job if he's not careful."

"Ok Jade. What are you gonna do when he gets back? You're not going to forgive him are you?"

"Well I'm certainly not going to move out. I guess we will continue to live at opposite ends of the house."

"I'd divorce that SOB in a heartbeat Jade."

"You know I'm not happy Rita but I have no

place to go and I'm not leaving until some kind of agreement can be met on settlement."

Ok, got her off the phone. I need to take a shower. Sometimes I think better while the hot water rushes through my hair and tensions are released.

Just as I stepped out of the shower, the phone rang.

"You awake?"

"Hi Bob. Yes, I was taking a shower but it's ok. He should be home today. I just don't know what time."

"Ok, I'll let you go."

One more time, at least I got my hair washed before the phone rang again. Feeling punchy I answered, *"Grand Central Station."*

"Do what?"

"Hey everyone has called today wondering when you will be home."

"That's why I'm calling. I am on my way back now. If the traffic doesn't hold me up, I should be home around 6pm."

"Drive careful then." With a slight pause before I hung up I asked, *"Hey, did you ever hear from her?"*

"No and I blew over twenty bucks on flowers for nothing. The florist wasn't able to deliver them. There's a guy living in the apartment of the return

address she had on the Christmas card- said he had been living there for several months now."

"She didn't put a return address on the Valentine's cards she sent. I still feel like all this is bogus. See you after while."

I might have been pushing it a little but, I wanted him to know that I still loved him despite all the crap we had been through. *"I love you."*

"Are you going anywhere today? I was hoping you would stick around in case she tries to call."

He just pretended he didn't hear those three important little words or perhaps he wished they were coming from Joygirl instead but there was no response.

"You're really pushing it you know. But I don't have any plans to go anywhere as I have no money or any access to any when you left. Besides, I would love for that bitch to call so I can give her a piece of my mind."

"Don't you start anything with her that would jeopardize me getting to talk to her."

"After the hell you have put me through, you don't have the right to tell me what to do about that bitch. After all this crap, she will be lucky I don't sue her for everything she's got when all of this is out in the open."

It was around 4pm when he called again. *"She*

just called. She is ok. What a relief."

Wait a DAMN minute. He has driven close to 2500 miles in four days, no sleep, barely ate, blew tons of money we really didn't have trying to find this no good wench and most likely has lost his job and all he has to say is, *"What a relief."*

CLICK...I hung up that time. I thought I would puke. Rita had asked me several times what I was going to do when he got back. Well, he made my mind up for me.

I carefully thought out and wrote down the conditions I wanted. No compromising here. This time I'm going to be the demanding snip and if they don't like it; then, he can sue for divorce and I will gladly clean his and his mom's clock.

Right on time, he rolled into the drive.

"I told you I would be here around 6 o'clock."

"My God, you look like hell warmed over. Was this woman worth it?"

"I feel like I look."

"I thought I would sit down and go over what she told me on the phone this afternoon."

"Let me finish picking up these cigarette butts and I will be right in."

"Looks like you tried to clean out the tobacco factory out here," trying to make a joke out of the situation.

Sitting down on the couch and he in his corner easy chair, I looked over at him without any expression. I could barely muster up any energy at all to hear this crock of crap but anyway, *"Ok, go ahead."*

With a deep sigh and it looks like he is about to cry his little heart out, he looked over and said, *"After she agreed to meet with me, she claims she and Edie (her roommate) got into a heated argument over meeting me. While she was taking a shower, Edie called Joygirl's brother, Steven, to come over. Steven called their mom who drove down and they took her car keys and cell phone from her to prevent her from talking to me or letting her leave the apartment. She was so upset that she cried herself to sleep in her mother's lap."*

"Gees what drama! What about all of Tuesday, Tuesday night and Wednesday?"

"She claims her mother took her out shopping Tuesday and out to dinner Tuesday night and she had no way to call me."

"This woman is supposed to be twenty two in July and her family still dictates what she can or cannot do? Are you now convinced you have been duped?

"NO, all of this is over the fact that I am still married. You're the problem," losing his temper and screaming to the top of his lungs.

"Well, since you have your dandruff up and you think I'm a big obstacle in your glorious plans for eternal happiness-I'm about to be a bigger one!"

"What's this?"

"It is a list of conditions to try and reconcile our marriage."

With his eyes rolling back into his head, *"What makes you think I want a reconciliation?"*

"The way I see it, our marriage is real and she is not."

"What's this 90 day thing you have written here? What is it for?"

"You remember telling me you and Joygirl wanted to meet but her supposed mother suggested at Thanksgiving you wait 90 days? I believe the reason was to see if the two of still had feelings after waiting?"

"Oh yeah. That's right. But I don't love you. I love her. And her love is worth waiting for."

"Well good then. You won't mind waiting another 90 days then! And, I mean the very first condition. If I catch you having <u>ANY</u> contact at all with her; I will sue her for alienation of affection and it won't be pretty. Seeing how I have plenty of evidence accumulated by your little road trip; my attorney could have a field day with this in court."

"When do these conditions take effect?"

"I will allow you one phone call"

Interrupting me, he blurted *"I promised her I would call her to let her know I made it home ok."*

"Make it brief."

"Do you think I could have some privacy here?"

As he sat down on the couch, I walked into the master bedroom but stayed within earshot. He spoke softly so I couldn't hear or so he thought.

"I love you," were his opening words. *"I love you and only you. You really had me worried. I can't believe you couldn't get word to me somehow that you were alright. I was afraid you might have wrecked in that bad rainstorm on the way to meet me. Yes, she is still here. That is the other reason I'm calling."*

There was a very long pause.

"Since I took off, she has made conditions I have to live by."

He read them off slowly.

"They take effect when we hang up the phone. Jade, pick up the phone now."

I barely had the receiver to my ear. She started screaming in "The Exorcist Voice", *"You no good, double crossing bitch. You can have your damn husband."*

"That's right. He is MY HUSBAND. So, why can't you do what YOU promised months ago and

leave us the hell alone. You say you have plenty of friends and you are seeing the "good doctor." Why can't you get involved with the people of your own community instead of F------ up our lives here?"

"It doesn't matter. I just lost my best friend over Tom. Edie and I got into a big fight and she moved out. If you would just give him the divorce, we could be happy."

"How can you think you can be happy with someone you have never met? How diluted is that? You never planned to meet him anyway, ever- divorced or not. You ARE NOT who you pretend to be and I will prove it or die trying- JUNE!"

CLICK....she hung up.

"Now look what you've done! You pissed her off without me being able to tell her goodbye. Let me call her back, please."

"Nothing doing. Let her be. She is NOTHING but a liar. She just proved it. My God Tom, it doesn't take a genius to see she has played you. In time, you will see through all of this and see she is ONE BIG LIAR."

He didn't catch that I called her JUNE, her real name.

CHAPTER 12

Life Goes On

A couple of weeks had passed since his road trip. The marriage was still terribly unstable but tolerable. One night, around 4am, I awoke from a terrible dream. I dreamed Tom was badly injured at work. For assurance he was alright, I called him.

"Oh it's you. I'm busy out in the plant. I can't talk now and he hung up."

If he had been out in the plant, it would have been so noisy I could barely hear him. Woman's intuition says- NOT... I called Byron, one of his coworkers in the other maintenance office.

"Hey Byron, what's Tom up to?"

He was very reluctant to answer until I said, *"Bet he is talking to the supposed young thang from Missouri."*

"I'm sorry Jade. I didn't know how much you knew and I didn't want you to find out this way. He has been talking to her for nearly two hours now. He has locked himself in his office and refuses to do any work orders. He brags on her all the time about her calling. Phil and I try telling him she is nothing but trouble but he won't listen."

"Byron, since when has he ever listened to anyone?"

"But it's getting serious here at work. He's gonna lose his job if he keeps this up."

"I'm surprised he still has a job after the little jaunt he took a few weeks ago. I guess he pushes his friendship with Page to the limit."

"He went out there for real? He hadn't said much around here except that he took a few days off to clear his head."

"The only thing that got cleared was his bank account! I'm not able to say much at this point but I WILL tell you that that idiot drove out to Missouri not knowing where she lived, what she REALLY looks like and only had a cell number to contact her with."

"What happened?"

"She stood him up!"

After a slight pause, we both laughed hysterically.

"That dumb ass. We tried to tell him he was F----
--- up but he wouldn't listen. Jade, we have both
tried to tell him you're the most understanding
woman in the world, that you love him like no other
woman in the world could. Just leave that SOB and
I'll dump Jessie and I'll make you happy."

"Byron, get real dude. You know I love every
inch of that SOB and I somehow will prove to him
what's really going on and hopefully before it's too
late."

"You know he has talked about quitting his job
here; said he was bored. He's got it made here, you
know?"

"It's her Byron. She has him thoroughly brain-
washed into moving closer to her and if he does that
you know his ex will never let him have the boys
ever again. He'll lose everything. Everything
Byron- all for pussy he has never had!"

Byron was laughing so hysterically. *"Oh girl,*
I'm not laughing at you but you can say the funniest
things."

"I have to laugh to get through this mess. Well,
I think I'll go have a smoke outside."

"He still makes you smoke outside? Piss on
him... I'd fire it right up in the house."

"Well at least I can smoke here now. When I
first moved here, I remember I had gone out back

and sat on the tailgate of his pick up. He came around the corner, slapped the cigarette right out of my mouth and told me I couldn't smoke on the premises. I told him if he ever did that shit again, he'd get it right back. I really don't like the smell in the house anyway but it doesn't give him the right to tell me I can't smoke.

Well dude, I am holding you up from work. I'll catch you later. Thanks Byron."

"Ok dudette. Hey you can still make me a peach cobbler sometime huh? Damn those things are good."

"Sure bud, anytime. Catch ya later, Byron."

My plan was to pretend I didn't know anything. Neither one of his co-workers would mention my phone conversation the night before. Tom wasn't exactly on their best friends list anyway.

One of the conditions in our 90 day agreement was for us to have sex everyday. Not that I enjoyed having sex with someone who loathed me so badly but for the satisfaction that it pushed Joygirl's button when he read that one condition to her.

Tom is like any other man- sex is sex as long as he gets some satisfaction out of it. But today was different. He seemed pre-occupied, perhaps feeling guilty about his hiding his conversations with Joygirl (yeah right). No, he is just worried he's gonna get caught and he knows I will follow through with my threat to sue her.

"What's the matter?" Like I really give a crap!

"I have been thinking about this for quite some time and I have come to a decision."

"Such as?"

"Things are not going well at work and I think I am going to turn in my notice. Do you think 30 days is enough?"

Damn, just when I think I have figured him out, he pulls this. I know my next remark is going to start an argument but what the hell. I have nothing to lose at this point."

So what's the problem at work? You have a gravy job and practically own your boss!"

Yes, I changed my mind about confronting him at this point to try and find out anything.

"Things have really changed at work. They are laying people off all over the plant."

"You knew when they created the electronics tech position and you moved laterally from mainte-nance that if the economy went South, your position would be cut. If they do that, you MAY have to go back to maintenance or they MAY lay you off."

"Yeah."

"So why not ride it out to see what happens? Either way, then you could draw unemployment until

you find another job. If you give notice, no matter what length of time, you know the policy; they will fire you on the spot and tell you pack your things and leave immediately."

"You think so?"

"I know so. You forgot when Dad had his heart attack and I had to find another job closer to home and I turned in my two week notice to the company, they let me go that day. They don't care."

"If you hadn't taken off from work and made the trip to Missouri I guess the only leverage they would have are your lengthy and excessive personal calls at work. They are cutting into your work performance and I guess Page is tired of putting up with it."

"But I'm not on the phone a lot now since I can't talk to Joygirl"

"So you're telling me you haven't spoken to Joygirl since the Wednesday night you returned?"

"No, I haven't. Not once."

"Really...Who were you talking to last night for so long?"

"What are you talking about? You mean when you called last night? I was out in the plant working."

"I guess you think I am some kind of idiot but if you want this to get down and dirty I can always

subpoena phone records to verify your conversation with Joygirl last night."

"The phone is in my mom's name and she won't let you have the bill."

"Oh hiding behind mama dearest isn't going to save your ass from a subpoena. Oh, she may not have said or done anything to her precious little boy about your road trip because she wants to protect your sorry ass; but there is nothing she can do about a court order but go to jail for contempt... Is this decision to quit your job motivated by working conditions or by Joygirl? It's less than three weeks since you made this agreement and you're cheating already."

"But I'm not cheating."

"Really...I sat outside your door at work last night and heard you talking to her. Making plans to leave the state for another woman isn't cheating? When are you going to realize you are being played a fool? Are you going to lose everything you have before you see what is really going on with this woman?

Whether we stay together or not, you need to think of your boys and not yourself for a change. Think about them. They are your future. What about them? Tom, have you totally lost your mind? If you think you have a future with this woman by just walking off and leaving your life behind, you are really f----- up. If nothing else, think of the age difference, it will never work."

"She said the age difference didn't matter. Ten good years with me would be worth it."

"Just ten good years? What does that mean? She planning on just ten years with you and then leaving? What happened until death do we part?

But the way I see it, she is lying about her age anyway so perhaps SHE only has ten good years left. With the sound of her voice, sounds like she has less than ten months!"

Trying to rationalize with him the past few months was pointless. Why should today be any different?

Quite agitated, he got out of bed and headed for the saw mill on no sleep.

When it was time to leave for work; he showered, dressed and left without a word.

I thought to myself, how long can he keep up this pace he is living?

"You doing anything? You feel well enough to drive the van down and meet me at the pizza place?"

"What's going on?"

Eating was the last thing on my mind so tea was

enough for me. And he hadn't invited me out to eat since the night after Joygirl and I chatted online the very first time and that was months ago.

"You were right."

"Ok Tom, we haven't spoken to each other since our fight this morning. What are you talking about?"

"They let me go. Last night without telling you, I turned in my 90 day notice. Page wasn't there so he didn't get it until this morning and when I went in I was told they didn't need me. I have my things to transfer over to the van."

"You never mentioned you were so serious about turning in your notice-only that you were thinking about it. Why couldn't you be straight up with me and just tell me what you did?

What about another job, insurance for all of us and not to mention the $600 monthly child support. How are we supposed to make that?"

"I still have some retirement I can pull out and I can work the saw mill until I find another job but I thought it best to turn in my notice rather than be fired."

"DAMN TOM.....Is this woman in Missouri really worth all of this?"

"Leave her out of this. She has nothing to do with this."

*"SHE HAS EVERYTING TO DO WITH THIS YOU **MORON**! You are acting so irrational and not thinking about anything but her. If only she would use her powers of persuasion to better use than screwing up people's lives. Who knows who else she has pulled this trick on. I know about your job inquiries for jobs in Memphis. You think you have it all planned out because you are familiar with Memphis from living there while in the service.*

You think finding one there will be better than trying to find one in that hick town in Missouri but you are forgetting two key elements.

How do you think your boys will feel about you moving? How do you think they will feel about being dumped for a woman...especially one you have never met in person?

They already don't like the idea that you planned to divorce me for someone you only know from the internet. They have more sense than you and they are only eleven and thirteen.

And there's Joygirl. There's the minor detail that you really don't know what she looks like much less what she is like in person."

Can you believe after making that entire spill, his only comment was, *"I know what she looks like. She sent me pictures, remember?"*

OH MY GOD!

Now with no night job; how was he planning to talk to his precious Joygirl? He has pressured me in the past to stop shooting pool Monday nights. Due to finances, I graciously agreed. Now I couldn't believe my ears.

"I've been thinking, maybe you shouldn't quit playing pool as it IS the only enjoyment you have and quitting may be too depressing for you. You don't ask for much anyway."

I started laughing so hard, tears were streaming down my face. This man was driving me to the nut house if I didn't have another stroke first.

"How can we afford for me to play pool after you just lost your job?"

"We will manage."

"What is this WE bit? You could care less whether I am depressed or not. The ONLY reason you want me out of the house is so you can have your quiet time with Joygirl."

"I'm telling you. I have not talked to her. I keep telling you this and you don't believe me."

"You can cut the act. I know all about the late night talks, the id's on the internet for you two to chat and I know all about the count down you have marked in your day planner. You underestimate me my dear. And so does she. Since you broke the agreement, I sent all the information I have to my

attorney for safe keeping. As soon as I find out her real identity, I am going after her for alienation of affection."

Busted, busted, busted! Two peas in a pod she called them. She called it right- liars and cheaters.

Suddenly, lover boy lost his appetite and was ready to leave the restaurant.

"I'll see you at the house." He said it so loudly and so angrily, customers looked up from eating to watch him storm out.

"Where are you going since you are no longer employed? Don't stay out too late talking to Joygirl on the phone. It is expected for you to perform to-night since you have plenty of time on your hands now......

Oh, tell Joygirl I said hello."

As soon as he walked out from under the over-hang of the restaurant door, the clouds literally fell out and poured rain. How befitting- certainly put a damper on his day!

CHAPTER 13

The Lie Continues

Well it was back to separate bedrooms while the boys were away. All the while, she kept up the farce of dating "Dr. Doug." She had Tom so torn up with anger. He always took it out on me or his parents.

He was impossible to live with. His screaming, ranting and raging just made me more determined to find out the truth about Joygirl and who she really was.

One night while at the computer, he was typing and smiling. I knew the two of them were chatting; but, I just ignored them. It gave them too much pleasure to see me angry.

Suddenly, the smile turned into a big frown.

"What's wrong?"

"That damn doctor just knocked on the door."

"Tom, I told you I found no such person in all of Missouri's registries or directories. He is another fabrication."

"If Edie works for him, he MUST be real."

"How do you know there is even an Edie? Have you ever spoken to her on the phone? Hold on...I'll be right back."

I returned with a notebook.

"What's the notebook about?"

"You didn't know this; but, since the first time I spoke with her on the phone I have kept this notebook with notes about all the people she's told me about; people I've spoken with on the phone and events. Supposedly, I've spoken to a Jami, a Laura and a Taffy but never with Edie who supposedly is her roommate and supposedly in the house quite often but she never will let me speak to her."

"Well you do have her cell, right? Maybe she doesn't have a house number?"

"Tom. Listen to yourself. When you were out in Missouri, supposedly the instructor of the class she was to attend (the day she stood you up) called her on her house phone while she was talking to you on her cell. You're making excuses for her. I wrote all the details down that day. I have nothing confused or mistaken."

"I'm f------ pissed. She messengered me that

Doug was at the door and now she won't answer my messages."

"Did you try to call her?"

"No, cause I know you would be pissed."

"Never stopped you before. Go ahead and call. I'd rather you call her than wear out the carpet pacing back and forth or being an ass to me."

I knew it was just another ploy to drive Tom nuts. For two days, she avoided him. He wasn't eating or sleeping. He was dropping weight and couldn't concentrate on anything. He had no patience and was snapping at everyone.

I couldn't take it any longer and called her. I hadn't spoken to her since the Wednesday he returned from Missouri. When she answered, it was cautiously.

"I'm not calling to cuss you out. I'm calling because I can't just sit by and watch him slowly kill himself with worry about you. I don't want you to interrupt me while I tell you something-ok?"

"Ok, what is it? I will stay calm."

"I don't want to argue with you simply for the fact, I don't have any energy. But I'm not leaving this place ever again and I am not giving him a divorce. Don't hang up on me either. Hear me out.

I'm not leaving until I can go back to work and can make it financially on my own. Then you two can do whatever you want.

So, stop playing games with Tom, answer your damn cell phone and talk to him. Agreed?"

"What's going on?" she asked rather perplexed.

"I really do love him and I hate to see him like this. He's not eating or sleeping. It is far too dangerous for him to be down at the saw mill working in his current state of mind. If you REALLY care about him, you will stop this game you're playing and tell him the truth before he accidentally kills himself at that damn mill.

I know some things on you. Things you should tell him yourself."

She butted in hatefully, *"So why don't you just tell us then?"*

Still remaining calm (hopefully the tone of voice will assure her I am telling the truth) I answered, *"In due time my dear, in due time when I have ALL the facts. Beside's he wouldn't believe me at this point. But you see, I am the one who has been with him for six years. I know him and love him unconditionally. You have only known him for supposedly six months. He will see you for the person you REALLY ARE in due time."*

CLICK...................I hung up on her.

For those who know me, the tone of voice I used is a threat that can be backed up. And she knew it also, for I had never used that tone of voice with her before. Am I worried she will tell Tom about our conversation? No, because she won't. She doesn't really want to stir up a hornets nest for fear I may really know something on her.

"Where have you been?" Tom asked as I entered the living room.

"I went outside to smoke a cigarette and to talk to Jennifer."

"Talk to whom?"

"My daughter, you know, Jennifer."

"Oh I thought you meant Joygirl and I have been trying to get her to talk to me all night."

"You know I call her Joygirl because Jennifer IS NOT her real name."

"Here we go again. Back to this shit again."

"No it's not back to this shit because there is no back to it. It's the same ole same ole- just a different day."

Closing down his laptop he pouted, heading off to his bedroom, *"I'm going to bed. It's been a bad night."*

After a couple of hours of staring at the stars, I tried to call Joygirl- no answer. I lit a cigarette and tried once more. WOW she answered.

"Hey, did you talk to Tom after we hung up?"

She sounded confused. *"I've been out with Doug. I'm trying to get over Tom and move on with my life. He is such a good man; working his practice all day and spending late night evenings with me."*

All the time, I envisioned this "person" describing all this to me with cartoon-like lovebirds and big red Valentines floating around her head.

"It's nice he can manipulate his hours to spend time with you."

Out comes the exorcist voice again, *"What do you mean by that?"*

"Just that you have failed to ever mention about him delivering any babies at night. I find it a little more than odd he's always with you in the evenings without any interruptions. Besides, I didn't call to fight with you. And if Dr. Doug IS there, I don't want to ruin your evening."

"No, it's ok. He went home; says he has an early day tomorrow."

"How convenient."

"What's wrong Jade. I detect some stress in your voice."

"I'm stressed alright. I am watching my husband that I wanted to spend the rest of my life with slowly die right before my eyes and all at the doings

of a complete stranger. A person he has given his heart and soul to but doesn't really know this person <u>*AT ALL*</u>*. And I KNOW you are not who you claim to be. It is a-l-l a fabrication-every last detail."*

"Prove it!"

"In due time- in due time"

"He will never believe you over me. I have made sure of that. Whatever you have on me; he would never believe anyway. So I am not worried."

CLICK…she hung up before I could answer.

It was this side of Joygirl I wished Tom had heard. She knows by the tone of my voice that I do know something.

"She told me what happened."

Now I know she didn't tell him of our conversation. I know she didn't admit to anything. So, I guess I better see where her imagination has taken her this time.

"Tom, what are you talking about?"

"The reason she never answered me after she wrote that Doug was at the door. You know how I always fuss at you for being in a hurry and running through the house?"

I just nodded at looked at him.

"Well she was running down the stairs and must have tripped because she fell down the stairs and was knocked unconscious. Doug couldn't get her to wake up to come to the door and had to get the super to let him in. They found her out cold in the living room floor. She said she must have hit her mouth on the steps as she knocked her front tooth out."

Now the first image I had in my mind after hearing this ridiculous story was Ollie the dinosaur character on television when I was growing up. It was all I could do to keep a straight face when I asked him if she went to the hospital to get checked out.

"I was so glad to hear from her that I forgot to ask."

"I wonder what the good doctor thought about you two messaging to each other when he found her?"

"What do you mean?"

"She is supposed to be seeing the good doctor to get over you. He may not like finding out she is playing both sides of the fence."

"Here we go again. You don't see any good in people, do you?"

"Not when they lie, cheat and manipulate other people. No I don't."

"You are so wrong about her."

"Really? So you're not the least bit upset that she is supposedly dating this doctor. Or? Perhaps you know she is lying about dating this guy"

"I'm not worried about the doctor because I know she loves me. I told her to go out with him because until I can get rid of you- I am stuck!"

Off he stomped to his bedroom. Later, I could hear him on the phone but couldn't make out what he was saying. It wasn't long before he hurried out the door and drove off without saying a word.

An hour passed and he hadn't returned.

I called Joygirl. *"What did you say to him to set him off like that?"*

"I just told him about me falling down the stairs and chipping my tooth."

"You told him you were knocked out and knocked your front tooth out."

"Yeah, that's right."

"That was our first conversation for this evening. I told him Doug laid down with me and we slept for a couple of hours."

"I thought you were knocked out? If you and Doug are in the medical profession, you know it is not good to go to sleep after being knocked out."

"Ok, you know your medicine and your point is?"

"You need to keep your stories straight is all. You're starting to slip old girl and I do mean old!"

She just laughed that same wicked, possessed laugh.

"Now what did you tell Tom to set him off?" I didn't tell her he was so pissed he left.

"Alright...Damn you're a nag. I told him in our second conversation that Doug told me I was a spoiled brat and needed a good f------- to straighten me out. So I threw myself down on the couch, closed my eyes and told him to f--- me now!"

Out of the blue she asked, "Is Tom skinny?"

"We've had this conversation before....don't you remember?"

"Doug has a 32 inch waist and I told Tom about him."

Damn no wonder Tom won't eat. Now she is practicing mind control on him through starvation.

THIS IS ONE SICK BITCH....

I wonder who else she has done this to?

There is no way I could even think about pulling such heinous acts such as hers. This bitch has got to be stopped. And I promised Tom – **I WILL GET HER!**

He never came back home that night. There is

no telling where he ended up.

The following Monday night when I came home from pool league instead of going straight to my bedroom; I quietly sat down on the couch in the living room next to Tom's bedroom. My hunch was right. At 2am, he called her.

He spoke of how worried he was about her. By the end of the conversation, I gathered she must have been at the emergency room with some sort of infection around a stomach incision. They continued to talk not really much about anything. He is mostly listening. She is so loud I can almost hear her side of the conversation with the phone to his ear.

"I can't trust you." he calmly said.

"WHAT? What do you mean you don't trust me?" She was screaming lividly.

Oh my, did he push a button or what?

He talks about my attitude and my tone of voice but I have <u>never</u> gotten by talking to him with that attitude. If I did, I was accused of being a bitch.

"I can't trust you to tell me when something is wrong with you. You won't call me."

"I guess I better get off of here and let you rest. I will try to call you tomorrow if I get a chance."

"Where is she?" I heard her ask.

"I guess she got in from pool and went to bed. I

was asleep when she came in. I better go."

I opened the door and turned on the overhead light. *"Oh don't hang up now. The conversation was just getting started. Not only are you a cheating husband but a rather stupid one too."*

He had the most dumbfounded look on his face. The ole deer in the headlight look.

"I've REALLY got to go now, bye."

I walked back to my bedroom without saying a word. He knew he had been busted. Following right behind me he started his explanation.

"I tried calling her earlier and she was at the emergency room. Someone else answered the phone saying she couldn't talk right now and then they hung up on me. I was simply trying to find out what was wrong with her when you caught us talking. How long have you been standing there?"

I never answered him.

"You know me pretty well, don't you," he mumbled going back to his bedroom.

Yep I sure do, thinking to myself.

Turning the television on for the morning news, they broadcast turbulent weather for Missouri all day and by the evening news he was pretty restless. He tried to pretend it didn't bother him but I knew better.

He wouldn't call her while I was awake so he

messengered her on the laptop. He waited what seemed forever but she never answered back.

The last forecast at 11pm was reporting tornados. He couldn't stand waiting any longer. He looked over at me as if asking permission to call.

"Go on and call. I can't stand you looking at me that way."

He dashed for the cell phone in his bedroom like it was his last lifeline. No answer- just voice mail. He paced the floor all night with the television on the weather channel.

It was days before she would answer her phone. And it was unbearable trying to put up with him. Once again, he tried to call her and she answered.

"Remember when you promised me Tom that you would never make me feel dirty and cheap?"

"Yes, I promised I would never <u>intentionally</u> do that. Why?"

"My brother has been on my case all day. Seems some cop friends of his have been listening in on people's phone conversations and just happened to listen in on one of ours. They recognized my voice and my friends' names I mentioned."

"What's the problem?"

"He claims they listened in on our phone sex

and it wasn't just one time. I feel so cheap and ashamed. I am so embarrassed"

What manipulative skills this woman has! Now, I have to wonder who really overheard their conversations in the past. I certainly don't believe the cock-eyed story she just told and it blows my mind that he does.

"I don't know what to do. My family will never accept you now."

Now if she had poured some tears in with that BS, it might have been a little believable. I just rolled my eyes with disbelief as he soaked up all the lies.

"I'm sorry Jen. I feel really bad. I'm sorry. We got carried away. I'll not call for a while. Let things cool down. We'll get through this. We will straighten this out, I promise."

"Tom, do you REALLY think they were listening?"

"It's a possibility."

"But you don't call at a regular time like you used to when you were working at night; how do they know when to listen in?

So that's the hold she has on you-phone sex?"

"No, that's not all of it. We talk about a lot of different things."

"Evidently, you must have told her your com-

plete life history as she knew things I had forgotten."

"She got me tickled one night. We were talking about country singers- she thinks Kenny is gay."

"Did she ever mention a guy named Robert?"

"I don't recall. Why?"

"She told me her roommate Edie got involved with a guy on the internet. He was married and from Ohio. Supposedly he left his wife and went to Missouri to be with Edie. But after a while they broke up and he went back to his wife in Ohio."

"She never mentioned it to me."

"She said Edie played a lot of Elvis when she was depressed but quite frankly, I've never heard anyone else or any other noises for that matter in the background when I am talking to her. Sometimes you can hear her hammering away on the keyboard and hear the messenger alert."

"Wonder who she is chatting with?" Now he has this insecure, bewildered look about him.

"I don't know but I would almost bet that this is nothing but a game to her and her friends."

CHAPTER 14

Slipping Up

Father's Day was approaching. It has been almost two months since I moved back and he was still infatuated with Joygirl. I had purchased two cards for each of our fathers. As Tom was signing his; he got a faraway look in his eyes.

"What's wrong?"

"It's the first Father's Day she will have without her dad. I was thinking how badly she must feel without him."

"She told me she was close to her dad and that she holds a lot of resentment towards her mom for dating so soon. But I don't believe any of her hogwash. It's all lies."

"Damn can't you cut her any slack at all? When did you talk about her dad?"

"The first day I chatted online with her she mentioned she lost her dad about a year ago. Then the other week or so when we were talking she mentioned it again but this time she babbled about a big house with acreage her family owned and her mom moved out of it into an apartment. You know me. I just let her babble so I could collect information for later."

"You're such a bitch. You know that- you're just such a bitch."

"Call me what you like but one day you just may be thanking me for getting it."

When Sunday arrived, I was looking forward to seeing my dad. It had been a couple of weeks when I saw him last and that was at his store. Tom always complained when I asked if we could go see my folks on a weekend. So I didn't get to see them as much as I would like.

We no longer had long distance on the house phone, so I grabbed my prepaid cell phone, the minutes were used up. I picked up Tom's cell from the kitchen counter. When I punched in a wrong number, I tried to clear it. His phone is totally different from mine and instead of clearing it; it automatically starting dialing a number. Then "she answered. I was so startled, I hung up. It was a phone card number. I caught him in another lie. He said he hadn't talked to her in several days- since the time she told him of their conversations being tapped. I am still laughing over that one. The phone indicated he called her just that morning and talked for over an hour.

"*You're constantly checking up on me- nosy bitch,*" he screamed to the top of is lungs.

"*It just so happened I wanted to call my dad to see what time he would be home for us to visit. But my cell phone's minutes were up. I simply picked up your phone to make the call as I didn't want to be bitched at for making a long distance call. What you're really pissed about is the fact that I caught you in yet another lie. I tried to give you the benefit of the doubt this past week and you got busted again.*"

"*Oh shut the hell up! You're not happy unless you find something to bitch about.*"

"*I didn't bitch. You're the one who grabbed your cell phone out of my hand and started cussing. Maybe, if you would stop cheating, lying and sneaking around and be the husband you vowed, you wouldn't have such a guilty conscious.*"

"*Well f--- you. I'm not going with you to visit your dad. Go by yourself bitch. Better yet, give me the keys. You're not driving anywhere.*"

I cried all afternoon. I missed seeing my dad but I would rather he didn't see me in this shape anyway.

The months of fighting was beginning to show on me too. I certainly didn't want dad to see me looking so badly anyway. I called him making up the excuse the car was missing badly. But you know how parents are. He could tell right away that something was wrong. I told him I was really disappointed because I hadn't seen him in a while and I missed my hug.

"Oh sugar, I will give you a big ole hug when you come to the office to pick up your paperwork. It's ok. I love you."

"I love you too daddy. You're my hero always, dad."

He didn't....... (Sorry, have to take a short break as I am crying) say anything. There was just a sniffle.

"Things will work out sugar. You can always move into the apartment at the store if you need to."

I had told dad what was going on with Tom as there were some days I was distant with relatives and I wanted dad to know it wasn't anything they were doing. It was the chaos in my family.

"I love you sugar. Cheer up now. One day, he'll come to his senses and things will work out. Men can be idiots you know. They think with the wrong head darlin'."

"Only when I prove she is a fraud. And I will dad. I will. If it is the last thing I do."

"If you need any help, let me know."

"Sure dad. But I have solved tougher mysteries than this one and I <u>will</u> solve this one too."

"You're a good detective. You can do this."

"I was just hoping he would have seen the light by now on his own. But HE IS thinking with the wrong head-you know that "getting to be an old man crap."

"Take care and dry those eyes now. Daddy loves you." And he hung up.

I hated dragging my dad in on all of this. But I am his only daughter and even though I'm the oldest at forty-nine; I am still his little girl. Dad never told me or my brother that he loved us until 1981 when I was twenty-seven and mom died from cancer.

He was a hardened military man and busy business man who never made time to express emotions. But he had changed. He was someone to confide in as a dad not the "colonel" as everyone calls him.

All day long, I thought perhaps "she" maybe did lose her dad and just maybe this was her first Father's Day without him—no matter how old she was, it's gotta be tough. Yes, I do have a compassionate side.

Tom went to bed early. I waited until he was asleep and I called Joygirl.

"I may not be able to stay on here long. It looks like it's going to storm soon. But I was thinking

about you today, it being Father's Day."

"It has been an extremely hard day. I nearly lost my best friend Taffy to a blood clot in her leg. You remember her? She's the friend I do everything with. She is my swim partner."

"They get her on blood thinners?"

"Yeah, but she doesn't want to take them. She doesn't want to be stuck taking it her whole life; being so young and all."

"Better to take it the rest of her life and it be a long one then dead-right? Did they say what caused it?"

"I hadn't heard yet and she really had us worried."

She just kept going on and on about Taffy and how concerned she was. For nearly 15 to 20 minutes and not one mention about the loss of her father last year. And not word about Taffy's parents.

"How are her parents taking the news? It was as if she didn't hear me or she was ignoring me.

"How are her parents taking it?"

"Huh, what did you say?"

"Her parents—how are they taking the news of their young daughter having blood clots?" By this time, I was a little agitated having to repeat the question for the third time.

"Oh" with a long pause as if she is trying to conjure an answer. *"Uh, they're, uh they're all dead."*

"My goodness to be so young and have lost BOTH parents—that's terrible! What happened?"

Well she may have thought she had me fooled but I wasn't buying that lie. Tom might accept her crap but not me. She was stumbling all over herself. Guess I was entering a part she hadn't rehearsed like everything else she had told Tom and I.

The weather started getting rough and there was lightning in the west over the mountains. I was on the house phone and I knew the call would show up on the phone bill but at this point after the big fight with Tom and not getting to see my dad for Father's Day, I really didn't care. Time to dog some more before the lightning gets closer.

"How's Doug?"

"He is such a good man. He is so good to me. But I don't know if I would be happy as a OB's wife-all that late night delivery stuff."

She never mentioned anything about night deliveries until the conversation we had and I mentioned he must have had a convenient schedule for him to be with her at night all the time.

She asked, *"Do you think it is too soon to be thinking about marriage at this point?"*

I know she asked that to push a button about a

Tom but I refused to answer her. I did notice that whenever I asked her about Doug she always started out with "He's such a good man." So rehearsed, she was like a voice activated recording whenever she heard the name Doug.

"Have you any brothers or sisters"

"Only true blood brother is about two years younger than I. No sisters, we were a small family. Remember, I told you he lives in Virginia."

"I have two older brothers, Pete and Saul."

"How old are they?

Now she has really stumbled up because she has forgotten that she told me about them already.

"Pete is fifty and Saul is in his thirties."

"Pete is fifty?"

"Yeah, he is living in Florida in a house my dad willed to me when he died last year."

This is the first time in the conversation she even mentioned her dad and it being Father's Day. When my mom died, the first Mother's Day was really rough. I cried all day. Even though my mom and I weren't close; I would send her a funny card and a serious, pretty card for that special day.

There is something very strange happening during our conversation. She is babbling more than usual but this time, she sounds as though she has been drinking or she is on drugs. She has told me a lot of this information before but if I pursue it; I just may fall onto the information Rita and I have been waiting for.

"Pete is my age."

"Oh yeah, he is. I forgot you are much older than, well, you know, what's his name?"

"Now don't bring up his name as our conversation is going so well up to this point. Why ruin it with tension."

"Yeah I know. I really appreciate our talks. You're a really nice person."

"Did you and Edie ever patch things up?"

"Not yet but trying. I had to buy a new fridge. The other one was Edie's and she took it with her when she left. The new one is not as nice as hers but it works good. Doug had talked about moving in with me. It would help us both with expenses and he is always over here anyway."

"Isn't his place bigger" Why not move in with him?"

"Oh............ (A very long pause) well he is losing the lease on his place so he mentioned us rooming together."

"Sorry I must have misunderstood you in our conversation a couple of weeks back. I thought you said he owned a house."

"Nooooo, I don't think I said."

OK now I am going to start to put some pressure on her about some things because the storm is getting closer and the lightning has intensified. Why not do the same with the conversation.

"How would you deal with trying to carry on a relationship with Tom and Doug living right under your nose? Or would you tell Tom it's really over this time?"

"I thought I would let you do that," she said with a sick, wicked giggle.

"Oh hell no...This is YOUR mess. I have enough crap to deal with when you upset him now."

She seemed to be amused that Tom and I are still fighting.

Changing the subject quickly she explained Doug would be leaving for a two week conference in California and she would be lonely.

"Guess you can put some extra time in at work to keep yourself occupied. WOW! The lightning is really streaking badly now-practically in our back-yard!"

"You must be getting the remnants of the storm that was through here not long ago."

"Most likely, when the weather channel shows all the bad weather you're having out there; it gets tense around here – especially when he can't get in touch with you."

I thought I would stroke her ego a bit to keep the conversation going.

"Well he needs to learn I have things to do here and can't talk all the time."

By this time, she is really slurring her words so badly I can barely make out what she is saying. I haven't heard any noises to indicate she is drinking so it must be drugs. I'm just going to keep pushing for information until I either get struck by lightning or she passes out!

"I meant to ask you. Back when I called for you one day, a girl answered the phone. When I asked to speak to Jennifer, they said I had the wrong number. Then when I called back, you answered the phone. Who was that that answered your phone on my first call?"

"I don't remember. Maybe you did dial the wrong number."

"Funny I hit redial and the same number dialed and you answered. At the time, you said she was changing the bandage on your incision."

"Oh that was Jami. She is a girl who helps me some. She is a friend of mine. She was changing the bandages where the incision is. I can't do it myself."

"You never told me what the surgery was for."

Suddenly, I hear a lot of voices and the slamming of a door.

"Who's downstairs?"

OH MY GOD! What a hateful tone of voice she used. And Tom calls me a bitch. She obviously wasn't expecting anyone to come home and she is really pissed.

"It's just us," a guy's voice said.

I never heard any activity, background noises or voices before-not even when she supposedly was working at the hospital or at the group home.

"Well be quiet, damn it. I'm on the phone. They want me to go fishing with them but I don't feel like it."

"The storm is getting worse here anyway and you need to tend to your company. I'll call Monday night after league and check on Taffy. Hope she gets to feeling better."

"Taffy? What's wrong with her?" She is really slurring her words now and is experiencing difficulties in remembering what we talked about. Damn I hate to hang up.

I hung up without answering her question.

CHAPTER 15

Review Time

"Jade, it's Rita. What's up?"

"Good Morning. How ya been?"

"Oh we're alright. You and Tom?"

"It's very trying right now but she is starting to slip up. She's starting to repeat information verbatim. You know. The ole, rehearse a lie until you believe it's true when you're a kid. Last night, she was tripping up badly. And tripping too! I don't know what drugs she was on but I would like to have some of them.

By the end of the conversation, I was wondering if she was going to pass out on me. When I questioned her on some of the facts she told me it was always me that got the facts turned around, not her."

"Are you still keeping that notebook?"

"Yep, even last night while I was talking to her. I was in the laundry room with the back door cracked open smoking, watching the storm roll over the mountains and had the notebook on the dryer taking notes all at the same time.

I even have stat notes on the different characters and filed them alphabetically. It's easier to cross reference the notes that way than flipping through the pages. She also can't hear me when I use the index cards verses the notebook."

"God, you're going through a lot of trouble."

"Look at all the crap those two have put me through Rita. Do you think my attorney really wants to sit and hear me when he can just use my notes if it goes to court?"

"Oh my God, are you telling me you're still willing to ride this out just to find out the truth?"

"All I am promising at this point is, I am going to prove this bitch is an imposter- you know it, I know it and I am going to prove to Tom what an idiot he has been. After that, we will just have to see what happens."

"Damn, don't get so worked up!"

"I'm sorry. My nerves are shot. Tom will be gone this afternoon. Can you come up and help me with some things?"

"Sure I can help. Anything to get this resolved so you can get your sanity and your life back."

I barely started sorting through all my research when she pulled in the drive and she lived over 50 miles away.

"Wow, that didn't take long."

"I was so anxious over what you had said that I couldn't get here fast enough."

"When's the court date for your custody case with your ex-moron?"

She turned laughing at the remark of ex-moron, *"Soon and I will need you to testify."*

"You know that's not a problem."

"I really want you there for emotional support and you always know how to take up for me and handle my attorney. You don't let anyone run over you the way they do me. Besides my attorney will listen to you!"

"He's too passive to handle a child custody case Rita. He comes off as a Mr. Clean and very un-intimidating. That is why he backs down to me and I am not even opposing counsel. He has yet to answer any of your questions concerning his strategy for court or contact any of your witnesses. You're paying him good money Rita with little or no results."

"You're right. I do let him get by with way too much. Mom fusses at me too."

As we are talking, we are walking back to my home office where I have spread everything out according to categories of friends, family, work, etc. When she walked in to the office, her mouth dropped open.

"Oh my God, how much stuff do you have here?"

"Only everyday of my life for the past seven months; I have every conversation documented, timelines drawn, cell phone bills that I could get my hands on, cards, letters, pictures, all the games they played with the date and times they played, maps of Missouri, and his hotel bills where he stayed when he left the last of April."

"So what do you need me to do?'

"You know the area Rita. I truly believe I know who this person is and we're going to prove it today! Everything will lead right back to this person," as I pointed to a name on the billboard written in big black letters.

"Oh wouldn't that just be too hilarious and outrageous."

"That is why I believe it to be true. Remember when we did the blocked call from your house? Do you remember the reaction you had when you heard her voice? There is no paper chase on a Jennifer Leigh Duncan from all the state of Missouri.

However, the initials do fit what I have written here. Everything points to this person right here."

"You remember the other night I told you I had talked to her again and she was slipping up?"

"Such as?"

"She supposedly was working at the hospital. When I told her I would let her go as she was probably busy; she said it was ok because she was through with the records."

"Records? What does she mean by records?"

"That's the funniest part. When I asked her the same question she said you know- records. When I corrected her by saying, 'You mean rounds and charts,' she said yeah charts."

"I see what you mean by slipping up."

"She's no RN Rita. I doubt anything that woman has said is the truth; except for one thing. The day of birth she gave Tom and I of July 8th but a different year matches this woman here as I pointed to the name again with the same initials. As small as towns are; it can't be too difficult to find out the real truth. When I mentioned that you and I were planning a trip to Farmington to visit your relatives; she actually invited us to visit her."

"She is rather bold isn't she?"

"She stated she would take us to a little bar she likes to go to in Ironton. This bar does exist Rita

and guess where it is? Right down the street from this woman right here," pointing at the woman's name on the board again.

"Joygirl was talking as if she lives in Ironton. When I called her on it, she realized she slipped up and then tried to change her story to meet her in Ironton so she and her friends could show us how to party. Then we could all crash at her friend's place which was just down the road from the bar. I asked her what her friend's name was, she stammered around."

"Wait a minute Jade. I thought she lived more than two hours away from Ironton?"

"Duh, do you see how she is slipping up now? Why would you want to drive way more than two hours away from a bar just to hang out? I know towns are small out there and spaced out pretty far but there are much bigger towns than Ironton that have bigger and better bars to hang out at.

Beside's that, when is the last time you heard anyone from OUR generation speak of doing something with their hair? Remember when I told you about the conversation I had with her when she said Dr. Doug was coming back from the two week convention and she hadn't done anything with her hair?"

"Wow, that's an old phrase. So where do we

start?" wrenching her hands together like a mad scientist.

"The only thing I haven't done is a directory search of Duncan in the surrounding area of Ironton. After we compile the list, I want to call some of them. The only chance we are taking here would be tipping her off through one of the relatives."

"I love this. She has put you through so much. You deserve the truth."

"Rita, I have given that winch every opportunity to come clean about her true identity. But she is so self-absorbed that she honestly thinks she has me fooled.

Like I told her, it involves six people on this side of the Mississippi River and only one of her on the other side. She has nothing to lose but we have everything to lose. If I don't get to the truth soon; Tom is about to sign away the rights to his boys and throw away everything that will be important to him. After the truth comes out, it will be too late. I can't let that happen.

He can't ruin his relationship with his boys over this tramp or sick psycho.

She has no regard for his boys or she wouldn't have talked with Tom on the phone so long during Daniel's championship ballgame back in the spring."

"Yeah, that was pretty selfish of her wasn't it? What kind of step-parent would she have made acting the way she does?"

"I would hate to think of subjecting the boys to someone of her caliber. You know, Tom and I had been dating quite a long while before I got to meet the boys. And even at that point, Tom was so protective of them I wasn't actually allowed to be introduced to them. I could only see them at a distance. I can't believe he would throw away his relationships with something like that."

Rita stepped over and wiped the tears from my face. My heart was breaking and there seemed to be such impossible odds of finding out the truth of this woman in time to save Tom from making some really bad decisions.

"This is so tough on you. I hate to see you go through this. Tom has no clue how much you love him and how much you are willing to give up to try and save him from something so stupid."

"I'll be ok as soon as I prove that bitch to be an imposter."

"I just realized you never told me how you caught on to them."

"Remember when the boys were out of school for Martin Luther King holiday? Beth had to be at

work and she let the boys spend the night at my house when Tom and I were separated and I still had my house I was living in then.

It was Daniel who told me about her."

"The youngest, the ten year old, right?"

"Yep, he asked me what heybaby636 meant. He said that there were times he would be sitting in his dad's lap playing kid's checkers and a blue box came up with that screen name written on it and then sometimes it was joygirl636."

"Oh my God," Rita's mouth dropped to the floor.

"Daniel said that he and Anthony had spoken to her on the phone around Christmas time. Daniel told me that they couldn't go anywhere without Tom being on the phone with her. Daniel got pretty upset one day in a store because they were supposed to be buying a DVD game for the play station. Instead, Tom seemed more concerned over what kind of cell phone belt clip Joygirl wanted."

"You really don't want to get your kids mad at you," Rita giggled. *"It comes back to bite you!"*

"To make a long story short, Daniel didn't appreciate Tom carrying on with this woman because Daniel knew I am Tom's wife. So now he is upset with his father."

"It just proves she really has no regard for the

*people involved in Tom's life including his boys.
Jade, now I understand why you are fighting so
hard. It is really for his boys' sake."*

*"I really don't care about myself Rita. I am old
enough to recover and move on. Brokenhearted but
not nearly hurt as badly as those boys will be if Tom
does something so ridiculous."*

*"So let's get back to work before Tom gets
back."*

*"Please call the people on this list. You know
the area. You could tell them you grew up around
there and are trying to find some old friends. Anything Rita, tell them anything. We have got to have
the truth now."*

The first few names didn't produce anything. I
was so antsy I walked into the kitchen to refresh our
teas. When I returned, Rita had the biggest smile on
her face.

"What's going on?"

*"Come look at this name I called, then look at
your list of names in your notebook. You did it. Jade,
You did it! You have gotten the goods on her."*

YOU BUSTED HER!"

Rita had tears running down her face. I just

slumped over in my office desk chair with disbelief. All our months of spying, searching, endless sleepless nights and long days to monitor the two of them and gathering what tidbits of information anywhere we could find it. We had all of it in front of us.

"What are you going to do now Jade? You have the information. What are you going to do?"

"How did you approach these people Rita? They won't tip her off will they?"

"Nah—it was a guy---young guy probably 17 or 18 years old. I told him I grew up in Farmington (since I know that area best) and I had lost contact with a friend of mine and dropped a few names like you told me.

It worked just like you said. You were right Jade. Damn you have figured her out. Oh, I told the guy to please, please do not say anything. I told him I want to surprise her."

"Surprise her is right...What did he say?"

"Oh, he said not to worry. He doesn't like her anyway. Says she is a bitch."

"Yep, we have the right person!!"

"He says that is a part of the family that doesn't socialize with Garrette because of her. I thanked him for the info and for his time. He said no problem and hung up. So what's your next step/"

"Laying low until the time is right."

"How on earth will you contain yourself after getting all this today? I would be bouncing off the walls and ready to turn the knife after sticking it to him, if it were up to me."

I laughed hysterically. *"Rita, contain yourself please. Just be patient my dear. Remember what I told Joygirl when I told her I would expose her- <u>all in due time</u>. I have waited this long. I can wait a little longer!*

CHAPTER 16

The Beginning of the End
July 17, 2003

"Have you heard from Joygirl?"

I was rinsing dishes off so it caught me by surprise. *"Come to think about it, it has been over a week since we last spoke. The last few conversations I had with her; she was slurring her words so badly it was difficult to understand her. Why?"*

"July 8th was her birthday. I sent her a birthday card and I have tried to call her but it says her voice mailbox is full. I'm worried about her."

The first thing that went through my mind was how jealous and hurt I was that he would send her a birthday card and never in five years we had been together had he ever bought me a single card of any kind. But now was the time to present the truth to

Tom as to Joygirl's real identity.

"Tom come sit down please. I have something to tell you."

"What is it? Is she ok? Is something wrong? Please tell me now."

"Just calm down and stay that way. Tom, we have been through a lot these past five years right?" I am trying to use my calmest, convincing voice

"YES"

"And you know that I said I would help and stand by you no matter what and I have done that despite your infatuation with this person- right?"

"YES"

"Have I ever lied to you?"

"NO, what is it? What is wrong with her? Please tell me what you know."

"Tom, it's time to take another trip to Ironton; but, both of us this time. I have the evidence to prove who Joygirl REALLY is; but, I knew the timing wasn't right to tell you. It is now."

Maybe it was reality slapping him in the face or perhaps the pain and conviction I expressed through my face and my voice but he sat calmly and listened to everything I had to say. No instant denials, no interruptions- he just sat and listened surprisingly calm.

"It's Friday and we really don't have anywhere to be. We don't get the boys this weekend and your parents' health is ok. So, let's take a road trip and get this settled."

I brought out all the paperwork I had collected in the search.

"Here is her name. This is her birth certificate. This is her home address. This is her husband's name and their home phone number."

"Her husband's name?" He looked at me in total bewilderment. *"Their home address and phone number? She's married? How can this be? How could she BE this person? When? As much time we spent together? How can this be?"*

"On the phone Tom, on the internet only-that's the REAL reason why she didn't meet you in April during your first trip. Here, dial this number and ask for her."

"But how can this be? How could she lie to me? She said she loved me and we could have at least ten good years together?"

"Tom, please, now is not the time to doubt my honesty. This is far too serious and this situation has hurt all of us way too long. It has nearly cost us everything we have. Please, just make the call."

I said it with such sincerity because I could see that in his own freaky, vulnerable way; he did love her more than he ever loved me as badly as it pained me to face the truth.

He slowly dialed the number still not believing any of it to be true. He first asked for Jennifer of which the man on the other end said there was no Jennifer that lived there. *"Can I speak to June please? Yes, I am a friend of hers from North Carolina. I am one of her internet buddies."*

You could hear the disappointment in his voice. As he wrote some information down, he turned and mumbled in shock, *"She's in St. Louis at Barnes Jewish Hospital."*

Now, I'm the one in shock. *"She's in the HOSPITAL?"* That would explain why neither one of us haven't heard from her lately. *"Ok, let's go pack."*

"Where are we going? Tom is so numb. He is just standing in the middle of the living room dazed and confused.

"St. Louis, of course. Hey, what was the conversation of internet buddies about?"

"When I introduced myself, he commented I must have been one of her internet buddies. She had a lot of internet buddies he said. How could she do this to me? If she is in the hospital and she's sick, why isn't he at the hospital with her? How could he

turn his back on her?"

"Who better to answer that question than you Tom?"

"How do you get that?"

"Why didn't you ask him? How easy was it for you to turn your back on me after I had my stroke in '02 and order me out of the house. How could you stand me up at the doctor's office while I faced the hardest, life changing news I have ever had to deal with in my life? How hard was it for you to turn your back on me?"

I started to the bedroom to pack as I was hell bent on going to Missouri some how, some way.

"Still in shock I guess is the reason I didn't ask. He sounded strange," Tom said as he followed back to the bedroom.

In case you didn't pick up on it, he didn't respond on answering how easy it was to turn his back on me while I was ill.

"How did he sound strange?"

"As if he had had a stroke or just thought and talked slow; sort of the way you did after your stroke and was in the hospital. Like you had to think about what you were going to say before you said it."

"Actually for me, I was just trying to put words together and learn how to speak all over again. So,

I wonder how many people she pulled this charade on. Believe me now?"

"How were you able to get all this information on her when the search I did revealed nothing?"

"Tom, if you were thinking straight, when you did the search for Jennifer Duncan and it revealed nothing, common sense should have kicked in and you would have known you were being duped. You just didn't believe it. Now, would you please go grab some clothes so we can pack? We'll call your mom to look after the dogs while we are gone, ok?"

"You're willing to ride all the way to St. Louis?"

"You made the trip before not knowing anything. Now we have the chance to find out everything."

We drove until we were completely exhausted and stopped at a hotel to rest. He was running on pure adrenaline but he knew that I tired easily so he finally took my health into consideration for a change.

I awoke to the sound of typing on his laptop. It was obvious he had not slept-too much on his mind.

"What time is it?" I asked still yawning from exhaustion.

"6:30 am, sorry I woke you. I couldn't sleep.

I've been up for a couple of hours."

My first thought, he was hoping she was on. But if she had heard that he had called her home and talked with her husband, she wouldn't be on. If she was, she would be using yet another alias to hide from the both of us. My second thought was who was he chatting with? Do I dare ask?

Questions like that in the past meant I was snooping and I didn't trust him. There's that word again- TRUST. Such a powerful word and no I didn't trust him and maybe never trust him again. What's the saying, "The predictor for future behavior is past behavior?" Enough said.....

So I will try a different approach. *"Honey, do you want me to take a shower first while you are on the computer?"*

"If you don't mind, please; I am looking up phone numbers and directions."

Wow! For the first time in months he didn't snap back sarcastically. Lathering my hair in shampoo, I thought how nice it would be to just close my eyes and let the water rinse away this hell I had been living. As horrible as it had been, the worst had yet to be discovered.

Eating breakfast and getting gas are just "normal" trip activities but today seemed to be prolonging the inevitable.

We agreed we weren't going to rehearse a lot of "what ifs" mostly for his sake. He still couldn't believe I knew who she was. There were a lot of miles traveled with little or no conversation about "it". We know each other all too well to assume we weren't thinking it though.

For me, it wasn't what he was going to say when he found out the truth; but, more the expression on his face. He has been so infatuated with this person that he was willing to give up everything in his life.

All for someone- this imposter- he has never met.......

I shook my head in disbelief as I stared out ahead. He looked over at me and immediately looked back at the road. He knew what I was thinking. He knew he had broken my heart repeatedly and deeply each time he pitched a tantrum about divorce. He just didn't dare mention it.

As complicated and as cruel the situation had gotten, we still were not fighting or screaming at each other. It was a time when he needed a friend, not a sparring partner.

Whenever we talked before, I always referenced us "on the East side of the river and "her" on the West side. Now crossing that river felt like crossing over a line drawn in the sand. My breathing had gotten shallow and my heart was racing. My brain was looping over and over what I thought for the last one hundred miles.

But he wasn't quite ready to face the truth yet so we boarded the riverboat for a little gambling. Stalling? Yes. Afraid of what the truth might be? Yes and understandably so. I waited patiently for him to get up his nerve.

And then it happened. He looked dead into my eyes. The very same way he did the first night we met and fell in love.

All I could mumble was, *"It's time to get to the truth."*

Finding the hospital wasn't as hard as we thought. It only took a few minutes. The elevator ride to the fourth floor seemed to take an eternity.

Walking the halls of some unknown place is like walking through a Halloween spook house. You never know what you will encounter around the corner and you certainly don't want to reveal the fear in your eyes if taken by surprise.

We located the room number but were unsure of what was going on inside. The room was packed with people. The woman was lying on her side facing the outside wall as if she were looking out the window away from the door.

I stopped by the nurses' station and asked if there was a woman by the last name of Duncan in room 2. When she shook her head yes, I asked if she would ask a family member to step outside to the hallway for me, please.

A very nice and attractive brunette met me. *"The family has gone downstairs to take a break. Can I help you with something?"*

I motioned for Tom. *"Please go downstairs and retrieve the information as I accidentally left it in the car."*

"We are from North Carolina and have driven to see June. When we spoke to her husband on the phone he stated she was in the hospital. He didn't mention she was so ill."

As the young woman was about to speak, a group of women rounded the corner of the hallway and the brunette introduced me.

"LEAVE NOW! I do not want you here."

"Can we please step outside and discuss this? I would rather not cause a scene here in the hospital."

She agreed reluctantly and I tried to calm her as we walked outside to the smoking section. I could see the catwalk for the parking garage and keep an eye out for Tom as I spoke to the women.

"I don't mean you any harm. I am Jade Morri-

son. Garrette told us she was in the hospital. He didn't mention how ill she was. We hadn't heard from her in a while and when we called her cell phone, her mailbox was full. We were very concerned about her."

"I know who you are and I don't appreciate you being here."

"Maybe not, but the fact is we drove all this way and we ARE due an explanation, please. Please explain who YOU are and why you are so upset."

I thought best to play stupid again.

At that moment, I looked up to catch Tom walking the catwalk into the entrance to the hospital. I didn't let on, allowing him time to go up first. We met him in the walkway with a total look of confusion on his face.

"Come in here, please." I motioned to what appeared to be a waiting room for that floor.

"This is my husband......"

"I know who he is. *I recognize his face. He is Tom. I don't know why you people just can't leave her alone and go back to North Carolina. Haven't you caused enough problems for my family?"*

With my blood boiling at that accusation but somehow containing myself, I snapped back. *"We came to get answers and we're not leaving until we get them."*

"My name is Taffy." She proceeded to introduce the other women in the room and then turned back looking directly at me. *"The woman in the hospital room is my mother. You know her as Joygirl and he knows her as Jennifer. She is 55 years old as of this past July, not 22 and has been married to the same man for over 18 years. She does not nor has she ever had a roommate named Edie. That is actually her nickname. She has never been an RN or even worked in a hospital."*

"So the two of you she calls her friends...."

Pointing to herself and the other middle- thirties woman, *"That is us and we are actually her daughters. The two kids she calls her niece and nephew are actually her grandchildren who are my children."*

"Did you just get out of hospital with a blood clot?"

She pointed to her swollen leg and replied, *"Yes. I nearly died from it. I know all about you and Tom. I read everything Tom and my mom had ever written to each other-every dirty little detail.* She turned and looked at Tom then back at me, *"Yes it was me you talked to that day you called my house asking if I knew a Jennifer Duncan."*

Tom just stood there motionless and quiet in total shock and disbelief.

"Why didn't you tell the truth that far back and save all this heartache?"

"It wasn't my place. I knew all about your business ventures and your failing marriage. What a joke it was to my mother. Mom often joked of making fools of both of you two. You're pretty stupid and pretty damn sick to travel all this far for someone neither of you know." She had this sick smirk to her face the whole time.

"Garrette didn't tell us she was this ill. We came out of compassion for the woman who was ill. We had no idea she was this sick-really. Yes, we appreciate an answer. Why would we have come all this way and NOT find out why and how she could be so cruel, so evil to pull the stunt that she did."

Tom held up the infamous picture of the young woman sitting on the side of the bed. *"Who is this?"*

"Oh my God, that is me when I was around fifteen!" Taffy shockingly said. *"How did you get that?"*

"Your mother sent it to me passing it off as her self." You could hear the anger and humiliation he felt.

"Taffy," touching her arm to get her attention, *"that was the first sign I knew your mom wasn't telling the truth. When Tom showed me the picture*

back in March I knew that picture was old by the harvest gold and avocado green striped sheets on the bed; that ridiculous looking hairdo and who the hell wears a guy's class ring anymore? But Tom didn't catch the signs. He was too flattered that she – a supposedly young woman - could be so nice to him - an older graying man - such as himself."

"I wish you two would just leave us alone." Looking back at Tom and pointing to me, "She is real. SHE is your wife. Go back to North Carolina where you belong and let my mother alone. I will call security if I have to."

"We wish you no harm. I just needed to prove to Tom that your mom was a fraud.

*You mustn't get so defensive and I wouldn't call security if I were you. I don't think you **really** want to explain to detectives why we had to drive all the way from North Carolina to find out why your whole family is involved in this scam.*

You see, it is a crime to do the things you and your mom have done to Tom. Your mom may be too ill to give us any answers but you're not in a position to threaten me "missy" seeing how you are an accessory to a crime. I don't want to lose my temper here and I don't make idol threats; but I suggest you start talking and talking fast."

I lost my own mother to cancer after battling it

for eleven years and my heart goes out for all of you. You not only have to accept her eventual death but also share some of the guilt for the disgust of what your mom has done to all of us with this charade. And....there is no telling how many others she lied to as well and how much you were involved in that too."

Taffy started to speak.

"Don't interrupt me, please. I forgive your mother. But I will never forget the heartache she caused and I hope I never run across another sicko like her."

"Would you please just leave, please, please just leave," Taffy realized then how shameful she felt or perhaps she felt ashamed that I could forgive her mother for the awful things she had done."

"Let's go Tom. I've heard enough of this crap anyway." Looking at Taffy, *"**YOU** have no idea how you and your mother's schemes have damaged my family. It just didn't involve me and Tom but also his two boys, my son and my daughter. Mine are old enough to understand but Tom's aren't. The relationship with his boys may **never** be the same. My marriage may not be salvageable from this. Tom lost his job. I lost MY house and damn nearly lost his. You're just as guilty as your mother if you could lie down at night and go to sleep knowing that*

your mom was such an imposter and a thief."

The look on Tom's face was as hollow and drawn as the day of his return from his first trip there. That's when I lost it and I pointed to Tom, *"So many miles he has driven not once but twice. Such disbelief, that he had been duped by your mother AND YOU. So many miles he had driven again and unable to meet the woman with the deep, raspy voice and the child-like giggle. Your mother carried this charade on since 2000. You can't tell me you didn't know anything about it even then. What a sick game to play on someone.*

But I guess you didn't think you would ever get caught. But I promised your mother I would call her hand when I had all the facts. I told her I would be here one day."

Pointing my finger, staring her down and in the most hatred voice I have EVER used I told her, ***"And I will deal with you and her about this. I promise you that too!"***

As we rode down the elevator, I was overcome with emotion. Finally, all my months of suspicions were proven to be right. Feeling cheated but relieved, I couldn't hold back. I started to shake, I broke down and cried.

"How can you be so calm? I asked with the tears streaming down my face.

"It is hurting me more that you know but it is hurting you more. You gave her plenty of chances to come clean about all of this and she wouldn't admit the truth. Deep down after that first trip, I pretty much realized she was lying but I didn't want to admit I was so stupid. I let my pride override the truth."

"Yes, I am very upset. I gave her plenty of opportunity over the past seven months to tell the truth; to admit her motive for pulling such a stunt. But she got too many kicks out of making fools of people."

There is really nothing anyone but her can say and she lay upstairs in a hospital bed dying.

Holding me tightly, Tom looked back at the hospital once more then nudged me to leave.

CHAPTER 17

The End

The ride back home seemed to hold more questions than answers. Can you imagine two trips to Missouri and back, over 2700 miles, searching for some kind of closure to this madness?

I should have hated them both at this point. A cheating, lying husband and a maniac woman from three states away; they had pushed me emotionally about as far as I ever imagined. Yet, all I could do was pity them.

I knew how empty and disappointed I was in my husband; but poor Garrette. He never had a clue his wife was "unfaithful" until the birthday card came in the mail for Joygirl's birthday. He thought she was on the computer for a cancer support group.

Guess that would explain why he wasn't at the

hospital with his gravely ill wife.

And my husband, who had the world at this finger tips- a good job, a wife who absolutely adored him, great kids and step-kids, parents that satisfied his every wish and command.

Perhaps, he had too much. Perhaps he never learned how to appreciate just how special people should be in his life. Perhaps he never respected life. A Godless man is like that...........

The 600 hundred mile ride home was lacking conversation. He was still in shock that he had been duped so easily. But he was probably more worried about how I was going to handle his infidelity. I was still thinking how to say how I felt.

I started about 150 miles into the return trip. *"I'm not going to lecture you how I told you so. You know I back up what I say. Rather I'm going to try and forgive you for she caught you at a very vulnerable time in your life. I am older Tom and I have seen this so many times with my friends' marriages. Women go through menopause and just mostly experience hot flashes and mood swings. Most men suffer so much more because it is their virility that is challenged to the fact they are getting older. She pulled out all the stops to manipulate you into loving her. The only thing I have never understood is when you heard that deep, smoky raspy voice, why did it not occur to you that she was not who she said she was? She definitely was no twenty year old!"*

"She told me she had bronchitis all the time from a childhood illness and I bought it. She made me feel sorry for her and she made me feel like her hero."

"Oh the poor pitiful rescue me act..."

"You're so independent and I admired that of you when I first met you. But, over time I felt like you needed me less and less. She made me feel important and needed. She told me she loved me and my heart just fluttered."

"But Tom, I told you I loved you and adored you and tried every way I could to be a good wife. I tried to show you every way I could that I loved you. I guess it wasn't enough."

"So where do we go from here?"

"We would be totally blind to think that this hasn't damaged our marriage. But, if we try perhaps we could learn from our mistakes."

I think he was hoping for a different response. I wasn't about to walk away now. Remember, I still had nothing. My home, my car- everything was gone. Where was I to go? I wasn't about to move in with my parents. So I stuck it out.

Fast forward from July '03 to November '04. I opened a pool room and worked really late nights. I called a friend of mine and got Tom working a third shift maintenance job. When he got off work, he would go by and stock the coolers in the morning to "let me sleep in."

The phone rings and when I answered the person would hang up. This starts to happen a lot. And the names are blocked on caller ID each time. Then one December day, the phone rings and it is a number I don't recognize. It is a local number though. When I answered, the woman hesitated for a bit then said she must have the wrong number.

I called the number back and a woman ten or so years older than I answered the phone. *"Someone just called my house and then they said they had the wrong number."*

Now for the bluff, *"but someone from your number has been calling my house a lot and hanging up."*

After an unusually long pause, you can hear voices whispering in the background telling someone to say something, *"Uh, it must have been my granddaughter. She must have dialed the wrong number."*

"Well please relay to your 'granddaughter' that her **friend** is married and please to leave him alone. DO NOT call this house again."

If a person wasn't guilty of such a strong accusation, they would take offense to that. But this person didn't say a word; just a long dead silence.

When I traced the number, it belonged to a woman's parents whom she lived next door to. This woman was in her late thirties, dark headed and drove a red car. She had a teenage son around the same age as Tom's oldest, Anthony.

That same number never came up again and the mysterious wrong number calls ceased until one day after Christmas.

This time a woman's name came up with a cell number. I never asked Tom who it was. I didn't have to. It was the same voice from the mysterious calls before. I already knew who it was and what was happening, again.

January 10, 2005 I awoke after a really long night at the pool room. Tom was already on the computer sitting in his infamous chair in the corner. I walked into the kitchen to get something to drink. I remembered years ago when we first lived together, Tom would always have a pot of coffee made. What a difference it was now. It was as if we were college roommates and it was everyone for him or her self.

With a big yawn, I looked over at Tom pecking away on the computer.

"What the hell is wrong with you?" he said in

the most hatred voice.

I just looked at him, turned and walked back to the bathroom to take a shower, quietly crying the whole way. Just as I started to step into the shower, I looked into the mirror. Who was this person I was looking at? My eyes were so blood shot from crying so hard.

I didn't even recognize the person I had become. I had tried so hard to please him that I totally lost myself and had absolutely no self esteem left. It was right then, that I made the best life decision I had ever made......

Taking my wedding band off with the diamonds from my deceased mother's ring, I calmly walked back into the living room and looked directly down at Tom.

"When I leave today to go to work, I'm NEVER coming back!"

You *really* didn't think I would stay with that BASTARD did you?

CHAPTER 18

Remembering June

She called two times after she got out of the hospital. She just said, "It was good to hear my voice."

June died August 22, 2003 at the age of 55.

She was survived by her husband, two daughters and their husbands, two brothers and a sister. She was preceded in death by one sister and her first husband.

The newspaper stated they had a private memorial service.

She, nor her daughters, ever explained why they

pulled such a nasty prank; a nasty prank that ruined so many lives.

I lost everything - the only home my children ever knew, my car and my life as I knew it.

There will *always* be more questions than answers.

Perhaps now that the book is out, maybe someone will come forward.

The one question still haunts me to this day.... **How many other lives were ruined by this woman?**

About the Author

Jade, a "city girl" approaching middle-age with two teenagers, thought she had finally found unconditional love with a "good ole country boy". But her life unraveled with his secret life of internet porn and chat room addiction. She had heard horror stories of the internet but thought she was immune to such ridiculous fantasy.

She kept a journal of his affair to work through her own anxieties; but decided to come forward to warn you that if YOU are in denial of the "pseudo" world of the internet-it just may cost you your job, your home, your car, nearly your kids----your life as you know it.

People are not always who they seem and the victims are not always children.